GRIMM'S · FAIRY · TALES
ILLUSTRATED · BY · ARTHUR · RACKHAM

A Peter Glassman Book

SEASTAR BOOKS • NEW YORK

Illustrations copyright © 1909 by Arthur Rackham
Afterword copyright © 2001 by Peter Glassman

The Arthur Rackham illustrations are reproduced with the kind permission of his family.

SEASTAR BOOKS
A division of NORTH-SOUTH BOOKS INC.

Published in the United States by SeaStar Books, a division of North-South Books Inc., New York. Published simultaneously in Great Britain, Canada, Australia, and New Zealand by North-South Books, an imprint of Nord-Süd Verlag AG, Gossau Zürich, Switzerland.

Library of Congress Cataloging-in-Publication Data is available.
A CIP catalogue record for this book is available from The British Library.

ISBN 1-58717-092-2 (reinforced trade binding)
1 3 5 7 9 RT 10 8 6 4 2

Printed in Hong Kong

For more information about our books, and the authors and artists who create them, visit our web site: www.northsouth.com

Contents

Rapunzel

THERE was once a man and his wife who had long wished in vain for a child, when at last they had reason to hope that Heaven would grant their wish. There was a little window at the back of their house, which overlooked a beautiful garden, full of lovely flowers and shrubs. It was, however, surrounded by a high wall, and nobody dared to enter it, because it belonged to a powerful Witch, who was feared by everybody.

One day the woman, standing at this window and looking into the garden, saw a bed planted with beautiful rampion. It looked so fresh and green that it made her long to eat some of it. This longing increased every day, and as she knew it could never be satisfied, she began to look pale and miserable, and to pine away. Then her husband was alarmed, and said : ' What ails you, my dear wife ? '

' Alas ! ' she answered, ' if I cannot get any of the rampion from the garden behind our house to eat, I shall die.'

Her husband, who loved her, thought, ' Before you let your wife die, you must fetch her some of that rampion, cost what it may.' So in the twilight he climbed over the wall into the Witch's garden, hastily picked a handful of rampion, and took it back to his wife. She immediately dressed it, and ate it up very eagerly. It was so very, very nice, that the next day her longing for it increased threefold. She could have no peace unless her husband fetched her some more. So in the twilight he set out again ; but when he got over the wall he was terrified to see the Witch before him.

' How dare you come into my garden like a thief, and steal my rampion ? ' she said, with angry looks. ' It shall be the worse for you ! '

'Alas!' he answered, 'be merciful to me; I am only here from necessity. My wife sees your rampion from the window, and she has such a longing for it, that she would die if she could not get some of it.'

The anger of the Witch abated, and she said to him, 'If it is as you say, I will allow you to take away with you as much rampion as you like, but on one condition. You must give me the child which your wife is about to bring into the world. I will care for it like a mother, and all will be well with it.' In his fear the man consented to everything, and when the baby was born, the Witch appeared, gave it the name of Rapunzel (rampion), and took it away with her.

Rapunzel was the most beautiful child under the sun. When she was twelve years old, the Witch shut her up in a tower which stood in a wood. It had neither staircase nor doors, and only a little window quite high up in the wall. When the Witch wanted to enter the tower, she stood at the foot of it, and cried—

'Rapunzel, Rapunzel, let down your hair.'

Rapunzel had splendid long hair, as fine as spun gold. As soon as she heard the voice of the Witch, she unfastened her plaits and twisted them round a hook by the window. They fell twenty ells downwards, and the Witch climbed up by them.

It happened a couple of years later that the King's son rode through the forest, and came close to the tower. From thence he heard a song so lovely, that he stopped to listen. It was Rapunzel, who in her loneliness made her sweet voice resound to pass away the time. The King's son wanted to join her, and he sought for the door of the tower, but there was none to find.

He rode home, but the song had touched his heart so deeply that he went into the forest every day to listen to it. Once, when he was hidden behind a tree, he saw a Witch come to the tower and call out—

'Rapunzel, Rapunzel, let down your hair.'

RAPUNZEL

Then Rapunzel lowered her plaits of hair and the Witch climbed up to her.

'If that is the ladder by which one ascends,' he thought, 'I will try my luck myself.' And the next day, when it began to grow dark, he went to the tower and cried—

'Rapunzel, Rapunzel, let down your hair.'

The hair fell down at once, and the King's son climbed up by it.

At first Rapunzel was terrified, for she had never set eyes on a man before, but the King's son talked to her kindly, and told her that his heart had been so deeply touched by her song that he had no peace, and he was obliged to see her. Then Rapunzel lost her fear, and when he asked if she would have him for her husband, and she saw that he was young and handsome, she thought, 'He will love me better than old Mother Gothel.' So she said, 'Yes,' and laid her hand in his. She said, 'I will gladly go with you, but I do not know how I am to get down from this tower. When you come, will you bring a skein of silk with you every time. I will twist it into a ladder, and when it is long enough I will descend by it, and you can take me away with you on your horse.'

She arranged with him that he should come and see her every evening, for the old Witch came in the daytime.

The Witch discovered nothing, till suddenly Rapunzel said to her, 'Tell me, Mother Gothel, how can it be that you are so much heavier to draw up than the young Prince who will be here before long?'

'Oh, you wicked child, what do you say? I thought I had separated you from all the world, and yet you have deceived me.' In her rage she seized Rapunzel's beautiful hair, twisted it twice round her left hand, snatched up a pair of shears and cut off the plaits, which fell to the ground. She was so merciless that she took poor Rapunzel away into a wilderness, where she forced her to live in the greatest grief and misery.

In the evening of the day on which she had banished

7

Rapunzel, the Witch fastened the plaits which she had cut off to the hook by the window, and when the Prince came and called—

'Rapunzel, Rapunzel, let down your hair,'
she lowered the hair. The Prince climbed up, but there he found, not his beloved Rapunzel, but the Witch, who looked at him with angry and wicked eyes.

'Ah!' she cried mockingly, 'you have come to fetch your ladylove, but the pretty bird is no longer in her nest; and she can sing no more, for the cat has seized her, and it will scratch your own eyes out too. Rapunzel is lost to you; you will never see her again.'

The Prince was beside himself with grief, and in his despair he sprang out of the window. He was not killed, but his eyes were scratched out by the thorns among which he fell. He wandered about blind in the wood, and had nothing but roots and berries to eat. He did nothing but weep and lament over the loss of his beloved wife Rapunzel. In this way he wandered about for some years, till at last he reached the wilderness where Rapunzel had been living in great poverty with the twins who had been born to her, a boy and a girl.

He heard a voice which seemed very familiar to him, and he went towards it. Rapunzel knew him at once, and fell weeping upon his neck. Two of her tears fell upon his eyes, and they immediately grew quite clear, and he could see as well as ever.

He took her to his kingdom, where he was received with joy, and they lived long and happily together.

The Witch climbed up.

Clever Hans

'WHERE are you going, Hans ? ' asked his Mother.
'To see Grettel,' answered Hans.
'Behave well, Hans ! '
'All right, Mother.   Good-bye.'
'Good-bye, Hans.'
Hans comes to Grettel.
'Good morning, Grettel.'
'Good morning, Hans.   What have you brought me ? '
'I 've not brought you anything.   I want a present.'
Grettel gives him a needle.   Hans takes the needle, and
sticks it in a load of hay, and walks home behind the cart.
'Good evening, Mother.'
'Good evening, Hans.   Where have you been ? '
'I 've been to Grettel's.'
'What did you give her ? '
'I gave her nothing.   But she made me a present.'
'What did she give you ? '
'She gave me a needle.'
'What did you do with it ? '
'Stuck it in the hay-cart.'
'That was stupid, Hans.   You should have stuck it in your
sleeve.'
'Never mind, Mother ; I 'll do better next time.'
'Where are you going, Hans ? '
'To see Grettel, Mother.'
'Behave well.'
'All right, Mother.   Good-bye.'
'Good-bye, Hans.'
Hans comes to Grettel.

10

'Good morning, Grettel.'

'Good morning, Hans. What have you brought me?'

'I've brought nothing. But I want something.'

Grettel gives him a knife.

'Good-bye, Grettel.'

'Good-bye, Hans.'

Hans takes the knife, and sticks it in his sleeve, and goes home.

'Good evening, Mother.'

'Good evening, Hans. Where have you been?'

'Been to see Grettel.'

'What did you give her?'

'I gave her nothing. But she gave me something.'

'What did she give you?'

'She gave me a knife.'

'Where is the knife, Hans?'

'I stuck it in my sleeve.'

'That's a stupid place, Hans. You should have put it in your pocket.'

'Never mind, Mother; I'll do better next time.'

'Where are you going, Hans?'

'To see Grettel, Mother.'

'Behave well, then.'

'All right, Mother. Good-bye.'

'Good-bye, Hans.'

Hans comes to Grettel.

'Good morning, Grettel.'

'Good morning, Hans. Have you brought me anything nice?'

'I've brought nothing. What have you got for me?'

Grettel gives him a young kid.

'Good-bye, Grettel.'

'Good-bye, Hans.'

Hans takes the kid, ties its legs together, and puts it in his pocket.

When he got home, it was suffocated.

'Good evening, Mother.'

'Good evening, Hans. Where have you been?'

'Been to see Grettel, Mother.'

'What did you give her?'

'I gave her nothing. But I brought away something.'

'What did Grettel give you?'

'She gave me a young kid.'

'What did you do with the kid?'

'Put it in my pocket, Mother.'

'That was very stupid. You should have led it by a rope.'

'Never mind, Mother; I'll manage better next time.'

'Where are you going, Hans?'

'To see Grettel, Mother.'

'Manage well, then.'

'All right, Mother. Good-bye.'

'Good-bye, Hans.'

Hans comes to Grettel.

'Good morning, Grettel.'

'Good morning, Hans. What have you brought me?'

12

' I 've brought you nothing.   What have you got for me?'
Grettel gives him a piece of bacon.

' Good-bye, Grettel.'

' Good-bye, Hans.'

Hans takes the bacon, ties a rope round it, and drags it
along behind him.   The dogs come after him, and eat it up.
When he got home he had the rope in his hand, but there was
nothing at the end of it.

' Good evening, Mother.'

' Good evening, Hans.   Where have you been?'

' To see Grettel, Mother.'

' What did you take her?'

' I took nothing.   But I
brought something away.'

' What did she give you?'

' She gave me a piece of
bacon.'

When he got home he had the rope in his hand, but there was nothing at the end of it.

' What did you do with the bacon, Hans?'

' I tied it to a rope, and dragged it home.   But the dogs
ate it.'

13

'That was a stupid business, Hans. You should have carried it on your head.'

'Never mind, Mother; I'll do better next time.'

'Where are you going, Hans?'

'To see Grettel, Mother.'

'Behave properly, then.'

'All right, Mother. Good-bye.'

'Good-bye, Hans.'

Hans comes to Grettel.

'Good morning, Grettel.'

'Good morning, Hans. What have you brought me?'

'I've brought nothing. What have you got for me?'

Grettel gives Hans a calf.

'Good-bye, Grettel.'

'Good-bye, Hans.'

Hans takes the calf, and puts it on his head. It kicks his face.

'Good evening, Mother.'

'Good evening, Hans. Where have you been?'

'Been to see Grettel, Mother.'

'What did you take her?'

'I took her nothing, Mother. She gave me something.'

'What did she give you, Hans?'

'She gave me a calf, Mother.'

'What did you do with the calf?'

'Put it on my head, Mother, and it kicked my face.'

'That was very stupid, Hans. You should have led it by a rope, and put it in the cow-stall.'

'Never mind, Mother; I'll do better next time.'

'Where are you going, Hans?'

'To see Grettel, Mother.'

'Mind how you behave, Hans.'

'All right, Mother. Good-bye.'

Hans goes to Grettel.

'Good morning, Grettel.'

'Good morning, Hans. What have you brought me?'

'I 've brought you nothing. I want to take away something.'

'I 'll go with you myself, Hans.'

Hans ties Grettel to a rope, and leads her home, where he puts her in a stall, and ties her up.   Then he goes into the house to his Mother.

'Good evening, Mother.'

'Good evening, Hans.   Where have you been ? '

'To see Grettel, Mother.'

'What did you take her ? '

'I took nothing.'

'What did Grettel give you ? '

'She gave me nothing.   She came with me.'

'Where did you leave Grettel ? '

'Tied up in the stable with a rope.'

'That was stupid.   You should have cast sheep's eyes at her.'

'Never mind ; I 'll do better next time.'

Hans went into the stable, plucked the eyes out of the cows and calves, and threw them in Grettel's face.

Grettel got angry, broke the rope, and ran away.

Yet she became Hans' wife.

Briar Rose

A LONG time ago there lived a King and Queen, who said every day, 'If only we had a child'; but for a long time they had none.

It fell out once, as the Queen was bathing, that a frog crept out of the water on to the land, and said to her: 'Your wish shall be fulfilled; before a year has passed you shall bring a daughter into the world.'

The frog's words came true. The Queen had a little girl who was so beautiful that the King could not contain himself for joy, and prepared a great feast. He invited not only his relations, friends, and acquaintances, but the fairies, in order that they might be favourably and kindly disposed towards the child. There were thirteen of them in the kingdom, but as the King had only twelve golden plates for them to eat from, one of the fairies had to stay at home.

The feast was held with all splendour, and when it came to an end the fairies all presented the child with a magic gift. One gave her virtue, another beauty, a third riches, and so on, with everything in the world that she could wish for.

When eleven of the fairies had said their say, the thirteenth suddenly appeared. She wanted to revenge herself for not having been invited. Without greeting any one, or even glancing at the company, she called out in a loud voice: 'The Princess shall prick herself with a distaff in her fifteenth year and shall fall down dead'; and without another word she turned and left the hall.

Every one was terror-struck, but the twelfth fairy, whose wish was still unspoken, stepped forward. She could not cancel the curse, but could only soften it, so she said: 'It

16

The King could not contain himself for joy.

shall not be death, but a deep sleep lasting a hundred years, into which your daughter shall fall.'

The King was so anxious to guard his dear child from the

'The Thirteenth Fairy.'

misfortune, that he sent out a command that all the distaffs in the whole kingdom should be burned.

As time went on all the promises of the fairies came true. The Princess grew up so beautiful, modest, kind, and clever

18

that every one who saw her could not but love her. Now it happened that on the very day when she was fifteen years old the King and Queen were away from home, and the Princess was left quite alone in the castle. She wandered about over the whole place, looking at rooms and halls as she pleased, and at last she came to an old tower. She ascended a narrow, winding staircase and reached a little door. A rusty key was sticking in the lock, and when she turned it the door flew open. In a little room sat an old woman with a spindle, spinning her flax busily.

'Good day, Granny,' said the Princess; 'what are you doing?'

'I am spinning,' said the old woman, and nodded her head.

'What is the thing that whirls round so merrily?' asked the Princess; and she took the spindle and tried to spin too.

But she had scarcely touched it before the curse was fulfilled, and she pricked her finger with the spindle. The instant she felt the prick she fell upon the bed which was standing near, and lay still in a deep sleep which spread over the whole castle.

The King and Queen, who had just come home and had stepped into the hall, went to sleep, and all their courtiers with them. The horses went to sleep in the stable, the dogs in the yard, the doves on the roof, the flies on the wall; yes, even the fire flickering on the hearth grew still and went to sleep, and the roast meat stopped crackling; the cook, who was pulling the scullion's hair because he had made some mistake, let him go and went to sleep. The wind dropped, and on the trees in front of the castle not a leaf stirred.

But round the castle a hedge of briar roses began to grow up; every year it grew higher, till at last it surrounded the whole castle so that nothing could be seen of it, not even the flags on the roof.

But there was a legend in the land about the lovely sleeping Briar Rose, as the King's daughter was called, and from time to time princes came and tried to force a way through the hedge into the castle. They found it impossible, for the thorns, as though they had hands, held them fast, and the princes remained caught in them without being able to free themselves, and so died a miserable death.

After many, many years a Prince came again to the country and heard an old man tell of the castle which stood behind the briar hedge, in which a most beautiful maiden called Briar

But round the castle a hedge of briar roses began to grow up.

Rose had been asleep for the last hundred years, and with her slept the King, Queen, and all her courtiers. He knew also, from his grandfather, that many princes had already come and sought to pierce through the briar hedge, and had remained caught in it and died a sad death.

Then the young Prince said, 'I am not afraid; I am determined to go and look upon the lovely Briar Rose.'

20

The young Prince said, 'I am not afraid; I am determined
to go and look upon the lovely Briar Rose.'

The good old man did all in his power to dissuade him, but the Prince would not listen to his words.

Now, however, the hundred years were just ended, and the day had come when Briar Rose was to wake up again. When the Prince approached the briar hedge it was in blossom, and was covered with beautiful large flowers which made way for him of their own accord and let him pass unharmed, and then closed up again into a hedge behind him.

In the courtyard he saw the horses and brindled hounds lying asleep, on the roof sat the doves with their heads under their wings : and when he went into the house the flies were asleep on the walls, and near the throne lay the King and Queen ; in the kitchen was the cook, with his hand raised as though about to strike the scullion, and the maid sat with the black fowl in her lap which she was about to pluck.

He went on further, and all was so still that he could hear his own breathing. At last he reached the tower, and opened the door into the little room where Briar Rose was asleep. There she lay, looking so beautiful that he could not take his eyes off her ; he bent down and gave her a kiss. As he touched her, Briar Rose opened her eyes and looked lovingly at him. Then they went down together ; and the King woke up, and the Queen, and all the courtiers, and looked at each other with astonished eyes. The horses in the stable stood up and shook themselves, the hounds leaped about and wagged their tails, the doves on the roof lifted their heads from under their wings, looked round, and flew into the fields ; the flies on the walls began to crawl again, the fire in the kitchen roused itself and blazed up and cooked the food, the meat began to crackle, and the cook boxed the scullion's ears so soundly that he screamed aloud, while the maid finished plucking the fowl. Then the wedding of the Prince and Briar Rose was celebrated with all splendour, and they lived happily till they died.

Red Riding Hood

THERE was once a sweet little maiden, who was loved by all who knew her; but she was especially dear to her Grandmother, who did not know how to make enough of the child. Once she gave her a little red velvet cloak. It was so becoming, and she liked it so much, that she would never wear anything else; and so she got the name of Red Riding Hood.

One day her Mother said to her: 'Come here, Red Riding Hood, take this cake and a bottle of wine to Grandmother, she is weak and ill, and they will do her good. Go quickly, before it gets hot, and don't loiter by the way, or run, or you will fall down and break the bottle, and there would be no wine for Grandmother. When you get there, don't forget to say " Good morning " prettily, without staring about you.'

' I will do just as you tell me,' Red Riding Hood promised her Mother.

Her Grandmother lived away in the woods, a good half-hour from the village. When she got to the wood, she met a Wolf; but Red Riding Hood did not know what a wicked animal he was, so she was not a bit afraid of him.

' Good-morning, Red Riding Hood,' he said.

' Good-morning, Wolf,' she answered.

' Whither away so early, Red Riding Hood ? '

' To Grandmother's.'

' What have you got in your basket ? '

' Cake and wine; we baked yesterday, so I 'm taking a cake to Grannie; she wants something to make her well.'

' Where does your Grandmother live, Red Riding Hood ? '

When she got to the wood, she met a Wolf.

RED RIDING HOOD

'A good quarter of an hour further into the wood. Her house stands under three big oak trees, near a hedge of nut trees which you must know,' said Red Riding Hood.

The Wolf thought: 'This tender little creature will be a plump morsel; she will be nicer than the old woman. I must be cunning, and snap them both up.'

He walked along with Red Riding Hood for a while, then he said: 'Look at the pretty flowers, Red Riding Hood. Why don't you look about you? I don't believe you even hear the birds sing, you are just as solemn as if you were going to school: everything else is so gay out here in the woods.'

Red Riding Hood raised her eyes, and when she saw the sunlight dancing through the trees, and all the bright flowers, she thought: 'I'm sure Grannie would be pleased if I took her a bunch of fresh flowers. It is still quite early, I shall have plenty of time to pick them.'

So she left the path, and wandered off among the trees to pick the flowers. Each time she picked one, she always saw another prettier one further on. So she went deeper and deeper into the forest.

In the meantime the Wolf went straight off to the Grandmother's cottage, and knocked at the door.

'Who is there?'

'Red Riding Hood, bringing you a cake and some wine. Open the door!'

'Press the latch!' cried the old woman. 'I am too weak to get up.'

The Wolf pressed the latch, and the door sprang open. He went straight in and up to the bed without saying a word, and ate up the poor old woman. Then he put on her nightdress and nightcap, got into bed and drew the curtains.

Red Riding Hood ran about picking flowers till she could carry no more, and then she remembered her Grandmother again. She was astonished when she got to the house to find the door open, and when she entered the room everything seemed so strange.

She felt quite frightened, but she did not know why. 'Generally I like coming to see Grandmother so much,' she thought. She cried: 'Good-morning, Grandmother,' but she received no answer.

Then she went up to the bed and drew the curtain back. There lay her Grandmother, but she had drawn her cap down over her face, and she looked very odd.

'O Grandmother, what big ears you have got,' she said.

'The better to hear with, my dear.'

'Grandmother, what big eyes you have got.'

'The better to see with, my dear.'

'What big hands you have got, Grandmother.'

'The better to catch hold of you with, my dear.'

'But, Grandmother, what big teeth you have got.'

'The better to eat you up with, my dear.'

Hardly had the Wolf said this, than he made a spring out of bed, and devoured poor little Red Riding Hood. When the Wolf had satisfied himself, he went back to bed and he was soon snoring loudly.

A Huntsman went past the house, and thought, 'How loudly the old lady is snoring; I must see if there is anything the matter with her.'

So he went into the house, and up to the bed, where he found the Wolf fast asleep. 'Do I find you here, you old sinner?' he said. 'Long enough have I sought you.'

He raised his gun to shoot, when it just occurred to him that perhaps the Wolf had eaten up the old lady, and that she might still be saved. So he took a knife and began cutting open the sleeping Wolf. At the first cut he saw the little red cloak, and after a few more slashes, the little girl sprang out, and cried: 'Oh, how frightened I was, it was so dark inside the Wolf!' Next the old Grandmother came out, alive, but hardly able to breathe.

Red Riding Hood brought some big stones with which they filled the Wolf, so that when he woke and tried to spring away, they dragged him back, and he fell down dead.

26

'O Grandmother, what big ears you have got,' she said.

They were all quite happy now. The Huntsman skinned the Wolf, and took the skin home. The Grandmother ate the cake and drank the wine which Red Riding Hood had brought, and she soon felt quite strong. Red Riding Hood thought: 'I will never again wander off into the forest as long as I live, if my Mother forbids it.'

The Bremen Town Musicians

ONCE upon a time a man had an Ass which for many years carried sacks to the mill without tiring. At last, however, its strength was worn out; it was no longer of any use for work. Accordingly its master began to ponder as to how best to cut down its keep; but the Ass, seeing there was mischief in the air, ran away and started on the road to Bremen; there he thought he could become a town-musician.

When he had been travelling a short time, he fell in with a hound, who was lying panting on the road as though he had run himself off his legs.

'Well, what are you panting so for, Growler?' said the Ass.

'Ah,' said the Hound, 'just because I am old, and every day I get weaker, and also because I can no longer keep up with the pack, my master wanted to kill me, so I took my departure. But now, how am I to earn my bread?'

'Do you know what,' said the Ass. 'I am going to Bremen, and shall there become a town-musician; come with me and take your part in the music. I shall play the lute, and you shall beat the kettle-drum.'

The Hound agreed, and they went on.

A short time after they came upon a Cat, sitting in the road, with a face as long as a wet week.

'Well, what has been crossing you, Whiskers?' asked the Ass.

'Who can be cheerful when he is out at elbows?' said the Cat. 'I am getting on in years, and my teeth are blunted and I prefer to sit by the stove and purr instead of hunting round after mice. Just because of this my mistress wanted

29

to drown me. I made myself scarce, but now I don't know where to turn.'

'Come with us to Bremen,' said the Ass. 'You are a great hand at serenading, so you can become a town-musician.'

The Cat consented, and joined them.

Next the fugitives passed by a yard where a barn-door fowl was sitting on the door, crowing with all its might.

'You crow so loud you pierce one through and through,' said the Ass. 'What is the matter?'

'Why! didn't I prophesy fine weather for Lady Day, when Our Lady washes the Christ Child's little garment and wants to dry it? But, not-withstanding this, be-cause Sunday visitors are coming to-morrow, the mistress has no pity, and she has or-dered the cook to make me into soup

A short time after they came upon a Cat, sitting in the road, with a face as long as a wet week.

so I shall have my neck wrung to-night. Now I am crowing with all my might while I have the chance.'

'Come along, Red-comb,' said the Ass; 'you had much better come with us. We are going to Bremen, and you will find a much better fate there. You have a good voice, and when we make music together, there will be quality in it.'

The Cock allowed himself to be persuaded, and they all four went off together. They could not, however, reach the town in one day, and by evening they arrived at a wood, where they determined to spend the night. The Ass and the Hound lay down under a big tree; the Cat and the Cock settled themselves in the branches, the Cock flying right up to the top, which was the safest place for him. Before going to sleep he looked round once more in every direction; suddenly it seemed to him that he saw a light burning in the distance. He called out to his comrades that there must be a house not far off, for he saw a light.

' Very well,' said the Ass, ' let us set out and make our way to it, for the entertainment here is very bad.'

The Hound thought some bones or meat would suit him too, so they set out in the direction of the light, and soon saw it shining more clearly, and getting bigger and bigger, till they reached a brightly-lighted robbers' den. The Ass, being the tallest, approached the window and looked in.

' What do you see, old Jackass ? ' asked the Cock.

' What do I see ? ' answered the Ass ; ' why, a table spread with delicious food and drink, and robbers seated at it enjoying themselves.'

' That would just suit us,' said the Cock.

' Yes ; if we were only there,' answered the Ass.

Then the animals took counsel as to how to set about driving the robbers out. At last they hit upon a plan.

The Ass was to take up his position with his fore-feet on the window-sill, the Hound was to jump on his back, the Cat to climb up on to the Hound, and last of all the Cock flew up and perched on the Cat's head. When they were thus arranged, at a given signal they all began to perform their music; the Ass brayed, the Hound barked, the Cat mewed, and the Cock crowed ; then they dashed through the window, shivering the panes. The robbers jumped up at the terrible

31

noise ; they thought nothing less than that a demon **was** coming in upon them, and fled into the wood in the greatest alarm. Then the four animals sat down to table, and helped themselves according to taste, and ate as though they had been starving for weeks. When they had finished they extinguished the light, and looked for sleeping places, each one to suit his nature and taste.

The Ass lay down on the manure heap, the Hound behind the door, the Cat on the hearth near the warm ashes, and the Cock flew up to the rafters. As they were tired from the long journey, they soon went to sleep.

When midnight was past, and the robbers saw from a distance that the light was no longer burning, and that all seemed quiet, the chief said :

'We ought not to have been scared by a false alarm,' and ordered one of the robbers to go and examine the house.

Finding all quiet, the messenger went into the

The Ass brayed, the Hound barked, the Cat mewed, and the Cock crowed.

kitchen to kindle a light, and taking the Cat's glowing, fiery eyes for live coals, he held a match close to them so as to light it. But the Cat would stand no nonsense ; it flew at his face, spat and scratched. He was terribly frightened and ran away.

32

He tried to get out by the back door, but the Hound, who was lying there, jumped up and bit his leg. As he ran across the manure heap in front of the house, the Ass gave him a good sound kick with his hind legs, while the Cock, who had awoken at the uproar quite fresh and gay, cried out from his perch : 'Cock-a-doodle-doo.' Thereupon the robber ran back as fast as he could to his chief, and said : 'There is a gruesome witch in the house, who breathed on me and scratched me with her long fingers. Behind the door there stands a man with a knife, who stabbed me ; while in the yard lies a black monster, who hit me with a club ; and upon the roof the judge is seated, and he called out, " Bring the rogue here," so I hurried away as fast as I could.'

Thenceforward the robbers did not venture again to the house, which, however, pleased the four Bremen musicians so much that they never wished to leave it again.

And he who last told the story has hardly finished speaking yet.

The Water of Life

THERE was once a King who was so ill that it was thought impossible his life could be saved. He had three sons, and they were all in great distress on his account, and they went into the castle gardens and wept at the thought that he must die. An old man came up to them and asked the cause of their grief. They told him that their father was dying, and nothing could save him. The old man said, 'There is only one remedy which I know; it is the Water of Life. If he drinks of it, he will recover, but it is very difficult to find.'

The eldest son said, 'I will soon find it'; and he went to the sick man to ask permission to go in search of the Water of Life, as that was the only thing to cure him.

'No,' said the King. 'The danger is too great. I would rather die.'

But he persisted so long that at last the King gave his permission.

The Prince thought, 'If I bring this water I shall be the favourite, and I shall inherit the kingdom.'

So he set off, and when he had ridden some distance he came upon a Dwarf standing in the road, who cried, 'Whither away so fast?'

'Stupid little fellow,' said the Prince, proudly; 'what business is it of yours?' and rode on.

The little man was very angry, and made an evil vow.

Soon after, the Prince came to a gorge in the mountains, and the further he rode the narrower it became, till he could go no further. His horse could neither go forward nor turn round for him to dismount; so there he sat, jammed in.

34

The sick King waited a long time for him, but he never came back. Then the second son said, ' Father, let me go and find the Water of Life,' thinking, ' if my brother is dead I shall have the kingdom.'

The King at first refused to let him go, but at last he gave his consent. So the Prince started on the same road as his brother, and met the same Dwarf, who stopped him and asked where he was going in such a hurry.

' Little Snippet, what does it matter to you ? ' he said, and rode away without looking back.

But the Dwarf cast a spell over him, and he, too, got into a narrow gorge like his brother, where he could neither go backwards nor forwards.

This is what happens to the haughty.

As the second son also stayed away, the youngest one offered to go and fetch the Water of Life, and at last the King was obliged to let him go.

When he met the Dwarf, and he asked him where he was hurrying to, he stopped and said, ' I am searching for the Water of Life, because my father is dying.'

' Do you know where it is to be found ? '

' No,' said the Prince.

' As you have spoken pleasantly to me, and not been haughty like your false brothers, I will help you and tell you how to find the Water of Life. It flows from a fountain in the courtyard of an enchanted castle ; but you will never get in unless I give you an iron rod and two loaves of bread. With the rod strike three times on the iron gate of the castle, and it will spring open. Inside you will find two Lions with wide-open jaws, but if you throw a loaf to each they will be quiet. Then you must make haste to fetch the Water of Life before it strikes twelve, or the gates of the castle will close and you will be shut in.'

The Prince thanked him, took the rod and the loaves, and set off. When he reached the castle all was just as the Dwarf had said. At the third knock the gate flew open, and when

35

he had pacified the Lions with the loaves, he walked into the castle. In the great hall he found several enchanted Princes, and he took the rings from their fingers. He also took a sword and a loaf, which were lying by them. On passing into the next room he found a beautiful Maiden, who rejoiced at his coming. She embraced him, and said that he had saved her, and should have the whole of her kingdom; and if he would come back in a year she would marry him. She also told him where to find the fountain with the enchanted water; but, she said, he must make haste to get out of the castle before the clock struck twelve.

Then he went on, and came to a room where there was a beautiful bed freshly made, and as he was very tired he thought he would take a little rest; so he lay down and fell asleep. When he woke it was striking a quarter to twelve. He sprang up in a fright, and ran to the fountain, and took some of the water in a cup which was lying near, and then hurried away. The clock struck just as he reached the iron gate, and it banged so quickly that it took off a bit of his heel.

He was rejoiced at having got some of the Water of Life, and hastened on his homeward journey. He again passed the Dwarf, who said, when he saw the sword and the loaf, ' Those things will be of much service to you. You will be able to strike down whole armies with the sword, and the loaf will never come to an end.'

The Prince did not want to go home without his brothers, and he said, ' Good Dwarf, can you not tell me where my brothers are ? They went in search of the Water of Life before I did, but they never came back.'

' They are both stuck fast in a narrow mountain gorge. I cast a spell over them because of their pride.'

Then the Prince begged so hard that they might be released that at last the Dwarf yielded; but he warned him against them, and said, ' Beware of them; they have bad hearts.'

He was delighted to see his brothers when they came back, and told them all that had happened to him; how he had

36

Good Dwarf, can you not tell me where my brothers are?

found the Water of Life, and brought a goblet full with him. How he had released a beautiful Princess, who would wait a year for him and then marry him, and he would become a great Prince.

Then they rode away together, and came to a land where famine and war were raging. The King thought he would be utterly ruined, so great was the destitution.

The Prince went to him and gave him the loaf, and with it he fed and satisfied his whole kingdom. The Prince also gave him his sword, and he smote the whole army of his enemies with it, and then he was able to live in peace and quiet. Then the Prince took back his sword and his loaf, and the three brothers rode on. But they had to pass through two more countries where war and famine were raging, and each time the Prince gave his sword and his loaf to the King, and in this way he saved three kingdoms.

After that they took a ship and crossed the sea. During the passage the two elder brothers said to each other, 'Our youngest brother found the Water of Life, and we did not, so our father will give him the kingdom which we ought to have, and he will take away our fortune from us.'

This thought made them very vindictive, and they made up their minds to get rid of him. They waited till he was asleep, and then they emptied the Water of Life from his goblet and took it themselves, and filled up his cup with salt sea water.

As soon as they got home the youngest Prince took his goblet to the King, so that he might drink of the water which was to make him well; but after drinking only a few drops of the sea water he became more ill than ever. As he was bewailing himself, his two elder sons came to him and accused the youngest of trying to poison him, and said that they had the real Water of Life, and gave him some. No sooner had he drunk it than he felt better, and he soon became as strong and well as he had been in his youth.

Then the two went to their youngest brother, and mocked him, saying, ' It was you who found the Water of Life; you

38

had all the trouble, while we have the reward. You should have been wiser, and kept your eyes open ; we stole it from you while you were asleep on the ship. When the end of the year comes, one of us will go and bring away the beautiful Princess. But don't dare to betray us. Our father will certainly not believe you, and if you say a single word you will lose your life ; your only chance is to keep silence.'

The old King was very angry with his youngest son, thinking that he had tried to take his life. So he had the Court assembled to give judgment upon him, and it was decided that he must be secretly got out of the way.

One day when the Prince was going out hunting, thinking no evil, the King's Huntsman was ordered to go with him. Seeing the Huntsman look sad, the Prince said to him, ' My good Huntsman, what is the matter with you ? '

The Huntsman answered, ' I can't bear to tell you, and yet I must.'

The Prince said, ' Say it out ; whatever it is I will forgive you.'

' Alas ! ' said the Huntsman, ' I am to shoot you dead ; it is the King's command.'

The Prince was horror-stricken, and said, ' Dear Huntsman, do not kill me, give me my life. Let me have your dress, and you shall have my royal robes.'

The Huntsman said, ' I will gladly do so ; I could never have shot you.' So they changed clothes, and the Huntsman went home, but the Prince wandered away into the forest.

After a time three wagon loads of gold and precious stones came to the King for his youngest son. They were sent by the Kings who had been saved by the Prince's sword and his miraculous loaf, and who now wished to show their gratitude.

Then the old King thought, ' What if my son really was innocent ? ' and said to his people, ' If only he were still alive ! How sorry I am that I ordered him to be killed.'

' He is still alive,' said the Huntsman. ' I could not find

it in my heart to carry out your commands,' and he told the King what had taken place.

A load fell from the King's heart on hearing the good news, and he sent out a proclamation to all parts of his kingdom that his son was to come home, where he would be received with great favour.

In the meantime, the Princess had caused a road to be made of pure shining gold leading to her castle, and told her people that whoever came riding straight along it would be the true bridegroom, and they were to admit him. But any one who came either on one side of the road or the other would not be the right one, and he was not to be let in.

When the year had almost passed, the eldest Prince thought that he would hurry to the Princess, and by giving himself out as her deliverer would gain a wife and a kingdom as well. So he rode away, and when he saw the beautiful golden road he thought it would be a thousand pities to ride upon it; so he turned aside, and rode to the right of it. But when he reached the gate the people told him that he was not the true bridegroom, and he had to go away.

Soon after the second Prince came, and when he saw the golden road he thought it would be a thousand pities for his horse to tread upon it; so he turned aside, and rode up on the left of it. But when he reached the gate he was also told that he was not the true bridegroom, and, like his brother, was turned away.

When the year had quite come to an end, the third Prince came out of the wood to ride to his beloved, and through her to forget all his past sorrows. So on he went, thinking only of her, and wishing to be with her; and he never even saw the golden road. His horse cantered right along the middle of it, and when he reached the gate it was flung open and the Princess received him joyfully, and called him her Deliverer, and the Lord of her Kingdom. Their marriage was celebrated without delay, and with much rejoicing. When it was over, she told him that his father had called him back and forgiven

40

him. So he went to him and told him everything; how his brothers had deceived him, and how they had forced him to keep silence. The old King wanted to punish them, but they had taken a ship and sailed away over the sea, and they never came back as long as they lived.

The Valiant Tailor

A TAILOR was sitting on his table at the window one summer morning. He was a good fellow, and stitched with all his might. A peasant woman came down the street, crying, ' Good jam for sale ! good jam for sale ! '

This had a pleasant sound in the Tailor's ears ; he put his pale face out of the window, and cried, ' You 'll find a sale for your wares up here, good Woman.'

The Woman went up the three steps to the Tailor, with the heavy basket on her head, and he made her unpack all her pots. He examined them all, lifted them up, smelt them, and at last said, ' The jam seems good ; weigh me out four ounces, good Woman, and should it come over the quarter pound, it will be all the same to me.'

The Woman, who had hoped for a better sale, gave him what he asked for, but went away cross, and grumbling to herself.

' That jam will be a blessing to me,' cried the Tailor ; 'it will give me strength and power.' He brought his bread out of the cupboard, cut a whole slice, and spread the jam on it. ' It won't be a bitter morsel,' said he, ' but I will finish this waistcoat before I stick my teeth into it.'

He put the bread down by his side, and went on with his sewing, but in his joy the stitches got bigger and bigger. The smell of the jam rose to the wall, where the flies were clustered in swarms, and tempted them to come down, and they settled on the jam in masses.

' Ah ! who invited you ? ' cried the Tailor, chasing away his unbidden guests. But the flies, who did not understand

42

his language, were not to be got rid of so easily, and came back in greater numbers than ever. At last the Tailor came to the end of his patience, and seizing a bit of cloth, he cried, 'Wait a bit, and I'll give it you!' So saying, he struck out at them mercilessly. When he looked, he found no fewer than seven

'Wait a bit, and I'll give it you!'
So saying, he struck out at
them mercilessly.

dead and motionless. 'So that's the kind of fellow you are,' he said, admiring his own valour. 'The whole town shall know of this.'

In great haste he cut out a belt for himself, and stitched on it, in big letters, 'Seven at one blow!' 'The town!' he then said, 'the whole world shall know of it!' And his heart wagged for very joy like the tail of a lamb. The Tailor fastened the belt round his waist, and wanted to start out into the world at once; he found his workshop too small for his valour. Before starting, he searched the house to see if there was anything to take with him. He only found an old cheese, but this he put into his pocket. By the gate he saw a bird entangled in a thicket, and he put that into his pocket with the cheese. Then he boldly took to the road, and as he was light and active, he felt no fatigue. The road led up a mountain, and when he reached the highest point, he found a huge Giant sitting there comfortably looking round him.

The Tailor went pluckily up to him, and addressed him.

'Good-day, Comrade, you are sitting there surveying the

wide world, I suppose. I am just on my way to try my luck.
Do you feel inclined to go with me ? '

The Giant looked scornfully at the Tailor, and said, ' You
jackanapes ! you miserable ragamuffin ! '

' That may be,' said the Tailor, unbuttoning his coat and
showing the Giant his belt. ' You may just read what kind
of fellow I am.'

The Giant read, ' Seven at one blow,' and thought that it
was people the Tailor had slain ; so it gave him a certain
amount of respect for the little fellow. Still, he thought he
would try him ; so he picked up a stone and squeezed it till
the water dropped out of it.

' Do that,' he said, ' if you have the strength.'

' No more than that ! ' said the Tailor ; ' why, it 's a mere
joke to me.'

He put his hand into his pocket, and pulling out the bit
of soft cheese, he squeezed it till the moisture ran out.

' I guess that will equal you,' said he.

The Giant did not know what to say, and could not have
believed it of the little man.

Then the Giant picked up a stone, and threw it up so high
that one could scarcely follow it with the eye.

' Now, then, you sample of a mannikin, do that after me.'

' Well thrown ! ' said the Tailor, ' but the stone fell to the
ground again. Now I will throw one for you which will never
come back again.'

So saying, he put his hand into his pocket, took out the
bird, and threw it into the air. The bird, rejoiced at its
freedom, soared into the air, and was never seen again.

' What do you think of that, Comrade ? ' asked the Tailor.

' You can certainly throw ; but now we will see if you are
in a condition to carry anything,' said the Giant.

He led the Tailor to a mighty oak which had been felled,
and which lay upon the ground.

' If you are strong enough, help me out of the wood with
this tree,' he said.

44

Pulling the piece of soft cheese out of his pocket, he squeezed
it till the moisture ran out.

'Willingly,' answered the little man. 'You take the trunk on your shoulder, and I will take the branches; they must certainly be the heaviest.'

The Giant accordingly took the trunk on his shoulder; but the Tailor seated himself on one of the branches, and the Giant, who could not look round, had to carry the whole tree, and the Tailor into the bargain. The Tailor was very merry on the end of the tree, and whistled 'Three Tailors rode merrily out of the town,' as if tree-carrying were a joke to him.

When the Giant had carried the tree some distance, he could go no further, and exclaimed, 'Look out, I am going to drop the tree.'

The Tailor sprang to the ground with great agility, and seized the tree with both arms, as if he had been carrying it all the time. He said to the Giant: 'Big fellow as you are, you can't carry a tree.'

After a time they went on together, and when they came to a cherry-tree, the Giant seized the top branches, where the cherries ripened first, bent them down, put them in the Tailor's hand, and told him to eat. The Tailor, however, was much too weak to hold the tree, and when the Giant let go, the tree sprang back, carrying the Tailor with it into the air. When he reached the ground again, without any injury, the Giant said, 'What's this? Haven't you the strength to hold a feeble sapling?'

'It's not strength that's wanting,' answered the Tailor. 'Do you think that would be anything to one who killed seven at a blow? I sprang over the tree because some sportsmen were shooting among the bushes. Spring after me if you like.'

The Giant made the attempt, but he could not clear the tree, and stuck among the branches. So here, too, the Tailor had the advantage of him.

The Giant said, 'If you are such a gallant fellow, come with me to our cave, and stay the night with us.'

The Tailor was quite willing, and went with him. When

46

they reached the cave, they found several other Giants sitting round a fire, and each one held a roasted sheep in his hand, which he was eating. The Tailor looked about him, and thought, ' It is much more roomy here than in my workshop.'

The Giant showed him a bed, and told him to lie down and have a good sleep. The bed was much too big for the Tailor, so he did not lie down in it, but crept into a corner. At midnight, when the Giant thought the Tailor would be in a heavy sleep, he got up, took a big oak club, and with one blow crashed right through the bed, and thought he had put an end to the grasshopper. Early in the morning the Giants went out into the woods, forgetting all about the Tailor, when all at once he appeared before them, as lively as possible. They were terrified, and thinking he would strike them all dead, they ran off as fast as ever they could.

The Tailor went on his way, always following his own pointed nose. When he had walked for a long time, he came to the courtyard of a royal palace. He was so tired that he lay down on the grass and went to sleep. While he lay and slept, the people came and inspected him on all sides, and they read on his belt, ' Seven at one blow.' ' Alas ! ' they said, ' why does this great warrior come here in time of peace ; he must be a mighty man.'

They went to the King and told him about it ; and they were of opinion that, should war break out, he would be a useful and powerful man, who should on no account be allowed to depart. This advice pleased the King, and he sent one of his courtiers to the Tailor to offer him a military appointment when he woke up. The messenger remained standing by the Tailor, till he opened his eyes and stretched himself, and then he made the offer.

' For that very purpose have I come,' said the Tailor. ' I am quite ready to enter the King's service.'

So he was received with honour, and a special dwelling was assigned to him.

The Soldiers, however, bore him a grudge, and wished him

a thousand miles away. 'What will be the end of it?' they said to each other. 'When we quarrel with him, and he strikes out, seven of us will fall at once. One of us can't cope with him.' So they took a resolve, and went all together to the King, and asked for their discharge. 'We are not made,' said they, 'to hold our own with a man who strikes seven at one blow.'

It grieved the King to lose all his faithful servants for the sake of one man; he wished he had never set eyes on the Tailor, and was quite ready to let him go. He did not dare, however, to give him his dismissal, for he was afraid that he would kill him and all his people, and place himself on the throne. He pondered over it for a long time, and at last he thought of a plan. He sent for the Tailor, and said that as he was so great a warrior, he would make him an offer. In a forest in his kingdom lived two giants, who, by robbery, murder, burning, and laying waste, did much harm. No one dared approach them without being in danger of his life. If he could subdue and kill these two Giants, he would give him his only daughter to be his wife, and half his kingdom as a dowry; also he would give him a hundred Horsemen to accompany and help him.

'That would be something for a man like me,' thought the Tailor. 'A beautiful Princess and half a kingdom are not offered to one every day.' 'Oh yes,' was his answer, 'I will soon subdue the Giants, and that without the hundred Horsemen. He who slays seven at a blow need not fear two.' The Tailor set out at once, accompanied by the hundred Horsemen; but when he came to the edge of the forest, he said to his followers, 'Wait here, I will soon make an end of the Giants by myself.'

Then he disappeared into the wood; he looked about to the right and to the left. Before long he espied both the Giants lying under a tree fast asleep, and snoring. Their snores were so tremendous that they made the branches of the tree dance up and down. The Tailor, who was no fool,

48

filled his pockets with stones, and climbed up the tree. When he got half-way up, he slipped on to a branch just above the sleepers, and then hurled the stones, one after another, on to one of them.

It was some time before the Giant noticed anything; then he woke up, pushed his companion, and said, 'What are you hitting me for?'

'You're dreaming,' said the other. 'I didn't hit you.' They went to sleep again, and the Tailor threw a stone at the other one. 'What's that?' he cried. 'What are you throwing at me?'

'I'm not throwing anything,' answered the first one, with a growl.

They quarrelled over it for a time, but as they were sleepy, they made it up, and their eyes closed again.

The Tailor began his game again, picked out his biggest stone, and threw it at the first Giant as hard as he could.

'This is too bad,' said the Giant, flying up like a madman. He pushed his companion against the tree with such violence that it shook. The other paid him back in the same coin, and they worked themselves up into such a rage that they tore up trees by the roots, and hacked at each other till they both fell dead upon the ground.

Then the Tailor jumped down from his perch. 'It was very lucky,' he said, 'that they did not tear up the tree I was sitting on, or I should have had to spring on to another like a squirrel, but we are nimble fellows.' He drew his sword, and gave each of the Giants two or three cuts in the chest. Then he went out to the Horsemen, and said, 'The work is done. I have given both of them the finishing stroke, but it was a difficult job. In their distress they tore trees up by the root to defend themselves; but all that's no good when a man like me comes, who slays seven at a blow.'

'Are you not wounded?' then asked the Horsemen.

'There was no danger,' answered the Tailor. 'Not a hair of my head was touched.'

49

The Horsemen would not believe him, and rode into the forest to see. There, right enough, lay the Giants in pools of blood, and, round about them, the uprooted trees.

The Tailor now demanded his promised reward from the King ; but he, in the meantime, had repented of this promise, and was again trying to think of a plan to shake him off.

'Before I give you my daughter and the half of my kingdom, you must perform one more doughty deed. There is a Unicorn which runs about in the forests doing vast damage ; you must capture it.'

'I have even less fear of one Unicorn than of two Giants. Seven at one stroke is my style.' He took a rope and an axe, and went into the wood, and told his followers to stay outside. He did not have long to wait. The Unicorn soon appeared, and dashed towards the Tailor, as if it meant to run him through with its horn on the spot. 'Softly, softly,' cried the Tailor. 'Not so fast.' He stood still, and waited till the animal got quite near, and then he very nimbly dodged behind a tree. The Unicorn rushed at the tree, and ran its horn so hard into the trunk that it had not strength to pull it out again, and so it was caught. 'Now I have the prey,' said the Tailor, coming from behind the tree. He fastened the rope round the creature's neck, and, with his axe, released the horn from the tree. When this was done he led the animal away, and took it to the King.

Still the King would not give him the promised reward, but made a third demand of him. Before the marriage, the Tailor must catch a Boar which did much damage in the woods : the Huntsmen were to help him.

'Willingly,' said the Tailor. 'That will be mere child's play.'

He did not take the Huntsmen into the wood with him, at which they were well pleased, for they had already more than once had such a reception from the Boar that they had no wish to encounter him again. When the Boar saw the Tailor, it flew at him with foaming mouth, and, gnashing its teeth,

50

They worked themselves up into such a rage that they tore up trees
by the roots, and hacked at each other till they both fell dead.

tried to throw him to the ground ; but the nimble hero darted into a little chapel which stood near. He jumped out again immediately by the window. The Boar rushed in after the Tailor ; but he by this time was hopping about outside, and quickly shut the door upon the Boar. So the raging animal was caught, for it was far too heavy and clumsy to jump out of the window. The Tailor called the Huntsmen up to see the captive with their own eyes.

The hero then went to the King, who was now obliged to keep his word, whether he liked it or not ; so he handed over his daughter and half his kingdom to him. Had he known that it was no warrior but only a Tailor who stood before him, he would have taken it even more to heart. The marriage was held with much pomp, but little joy, and a King was made out of a Tailor.

After a time the young Queen heard her husband talking in his sleep, and saying, ' Apprentice, bring me the waistcoat, and patch the trousers, or I will break the yard measure over your head.' So in this manner she discovered the young gentleman's origin. In the morning she complained to the King, and begged him to rid her of a husband who was nothing more than a Tailor.

The King comforted her, and said, ' To-night, leave your bedroom door open. My servants shall stand outside, and when he is asleep they shall go in and bind him. They shall then carry him away, and put him on board a ship which will take him far away.'

The lady was satisfied with this ; but the Tailor's armour-bearer, who was attached to his young lord, told him the whole plot.

' I will put a stop to their plan,' said the Tailor.

At night he went to bed as usual with his wife. When she thought he was asleep, she got up, opened the door, and went to bed again. The Tailor, who had only pretended to be asleep, began to cry out in a clear voice, ' Apprentice, bring me the waistcoat, and you patch the trousers, or I will break

52

the yard measure over your head. I have slain seven at a blow, killed two Giants, led captive a Unicorn, and caught a Boar ; should I be afraid of those who are standing outside my chamber door ? '

When they heard the Tailor speaking like this, the servants were overcome by fear, and ran away as if wild animals were after them, and none of them would venture near him again.

So the Tailor remained a King till the day of his death.

The Goosegirl

THERE was once an old Queen whose husband had been dead for many years, and she had a very beautiful daughter. When she grew up she was betrothed to a Prince in a distant country. When the time came for the maiden to be sent into this distant country to be married, the old Queen packed up quantities of clothes and jewels, gold and silver, cups and ornaments, and, in fact, everything suitable to a royal outfit, for she loved her daughter very dearly.

She also sent a Waiting-woman to travel with her, and to put her hand into that of the bridegroom. They each had a horse. The Princess's horse was called Falada, and it could speak.

When the hour of departure came, the old Queen went to her bedroom, and with a sharp little knife cut her finger and made it bleed. Then she held a piece of white cambric under it, and let three drops of blood fall on to it. This cambric she gave to her daughter, and said, ' Dear child, take good care of this; it will stand you in good stead on the journey.' They then bade each other a sorrowful farewell. The Princess hid the piece of cambric in her bosom, mounted her horse, and set out to her bridegroom's country.

When they had ridden for a time the Princess became very thirsty, and said to the Waiting-woman, ' Get down and fetch me some water in my cup from the stream. I must have something to drink.'

' If you are thirsty,' said the Waiting-woman, ' dismount yourself, lie down by the water and drink. I don't choose to be your servant.'

So, in her great thirst, the Princess dismounted and stooped down to the stream and drank, as she might not have her golden cup. The poor Princess said, 'Alas!' and the drops of blood answered, 'If your mother knew this, it would break her heart.'

The royal bride was humble, so she said nothing, but mounted her horse again. Then they rode several miles further; but the day was warm, the sun was scorching, and the Princess was soon thirsty again.

When they reached a river she called out again to her Waiting-woman, 'Get down, and give me some water in my golden cup!'

She had forgotten all about the rude words which had been said to her. But the Waiting-woman answered more haughtily than ever, 'If you want to drink, get the water for yourself. I won't be your servant.'

Being very thirsty, the Princess dismounted, and knelt by the flowing water. She cried, and said, 'Ah me!' and the drops of blood answered, 'If your mother knew this it would break her heart.'

While she stooped over the water to drink, the piece of cambric with the drops of blood on it fell out of her bosom, and floated away on the stream; but she never noticed this in her great fear. The Waiting-woman, however, had seen it, and rejoiced at getting more power over the bride, who, by losing the drops of blood, had become weak and powerless.

Now, when she was about to mount her horse Falada again, the Waiting-woman said, 'By rights, Falada belongs to me; this jade will do for you!'

The poor little Princess was obliged to give way. Then the Waiting-woman, in a harsh voice, ordered her to take off her royal robes, and to put on her own mean garments. Finally, she forced her to swear before heaven that she would not tell a creature at the Court what had taken place. Had she not taken the oath she would have been killed on the spot. But Falada saw all this and marked it.

The Waiting-woman then mounted Falada and put the real bride on her poor jade, and they continued their journey.

There was great rejoicing when they arrived at the castle. The Prince hurried towards them, and lifted the Waiting-woman from her horse, thinking she was his bride. She was led upstairs, but the real Princess had to stay below.

The old King looked out of the window and saw the delicate, pretty little creature standing in the courtyard; so he went to the bridal apartments and asked the bride about her companion, who was left standing in the courtyard, and wished to know who she was.

'I picked her up on the way, and brought her with me for company. Give the girl something to do to keep her from idling.'

But the old King had no work for her, and could not think of anything. At last he said, 'I have a little lad who looks after the geese; she may help him.'

The boy was called little Conrad, and the real bride was sent with him to look after the geese.

Soon after, the false bride said to the Prince, 'Dear husband, I pray you do me a favour.'

He answered, 'That will I gladly.'

'Well, then, let the knacker be called to cut off the head of the horse I rode; it angered me on the way.'

Really, she was afraid that the horse would speak, and tell of her treatment of the Princess. So it was settled, and the faithful Falada had to die.

When this came to the ear of the real Princess, she promised the knacker a piece of gold if he would do her a slight service. There was a great dark gateway to the town, through which she had to pass every morning and evening. 'Would he nail up Falada's head in this gateway, so that she might see him as she passed?'

The knacker promised to do as she wished, and when the horse's head was cut off, he hung it up in the dark gateway.

56

In the early morning, when she and Conrad went through the gateway, she said in passing—

'Alas! dear Falada, there thou hangest.'

And the Head answered—

'Alas! Queen's daughter, there thou gangest.
If thy mother knew thy fate,
Her heart would break with grief so great.'

Then they passed on out of the town, right into the fields, with the geese. When they reached the meadow, the Princess sat down on the grass and let down her hair. It shone like pure gold, and when little Conrad saw it, he was so delighted that he wanted to pluck some out; but she said—

'Blow, blow, little breeze,
And Conrad's hat seize.
Let him join in the chase
While away it is whirled,
Till my tresses are curled
And I rest in my place.'

Then a strong wind sprang up, which blew away Conrad's hat right over the fields, and he had to run after it. When he came back, she had finished combing her hair, and it was all put up again; so he could not get a single hair. This made him very sulky, and he would not say another word to her. And they tended the geese till evening, when they went home.

Next morning, when they passed under the gateway, the Princess said—

'Alas! dear Falada, there thou hangest.'

Falada answered :—

'Alas! Queen's daughter, there thou gangest.
If thy mother knew thy fate,
Her heart would break with grief so great.'

57

Again, when they reached the meadows, the Princess undid her hair and began combing it. Conrad ran to pluck some out; but she said quickly—

> Blow, blow, little breeze,
> And Conrad's hat seize.
> Let him join in the chase
> While away it is whirled,
> Till my tresses are curled
> And I rest in my place.'

The wind sprang up and blew Conrad's hat far away over the fields, and he had to run after it. When he came back the hair was all put up again, and he could not pull a single hair out. And they tended the geese till the evening. When they got home Conrad went to the old King, and said, 'I won't tend the geese with that maiden again.'

'Why not?' asked the King.

'Oh, she vexes me every day.'

The old King then ordered him to say what she did to vex him.

Conrad said, 'In the morning, when we pass under the dark gateway with the geese, she talks to a horse's head which is hung up on the wall. She says—

> 'Alas! Falada, there thou hangest,'

and the Head answers—

> 'Alas! Queen's daughter, there thou gangest.
> If thy mother knew thy fate,
> Her heart would break with grief so great.'

Then Conrad went on to tell the King all that happened in the meadow, and how he had to run after his hat in the wind.

The old King ordered Conrad to go out next day as usual. Then he placed himself behind the dark gateway, and heard the Princess speaking to Falada's head. He also followed her into the field, and hid himself behind a bush, and with his own eyes he saw the Goosegirl and the lad come driving

Blow, blow, little breeze,
And Conrad's hat seize.

the geese into the field. Then, after a time, he saw the girl let down her hair, which glittered in the sun. Directly after this, she said—

'Blow, blow, little breeze,
And Conrad's hat seize.
Let him join in the chase
While away it is whirled,
Till my tresses are curled
And I rest in my place.'

Then came a puff of wind, which carried off Conrad's hat and he had to run after it. While he was away, the maiden combed and did up her hair; and all this the old King observed. Thereupon he went away unnoticed; and in the evening, when the Goosegirl came home, he called her aside and asked why she did all these things.

'That I may not tell you, nor may I tell any human creature; for I have sworn it under the open sky, because if I had not done so I should have lost my life.'

He pressed her sorely, and gave her no peace, but he could get nothing out of her. Then he said, 'If you won't tell me, then tell your sorrows to the iron stove there'; and he went away.

She crept up to the stove, and, beginning to weep and lament, unburdened her heart to it, and said: 'Here I am, forsaken by all the world, and yet I am a Princess. A false Waiting-woman brought me to such a pass that I had to take off my royal robes. Then she took my place with my bride-groom, while I have to do mean service as a Goosegirl. If my mother knew it she would break her heart.'

The old King stood outside by the pipes of the stove, and heard all that she said. Then he came back, and told her to go away from the stove. He caused royal robes to be put upon her, and her beauty was a marvel. The old King called his son, and told him that he had a false bride—she was only a Waiting-woman; but the true bride was here, the so-called Goosegirl.

60

The young Prince was charmed with her youth and beauty. A great banquet was prepared, to which all the courtiers and good friends were bidden. The bridegroom sat at the head of the table, with the Princess on one side and the Waiting-Woman at the other; but she was dazzled, and did not recognise the Princess in her brilliant apparel.

When they had eaten and drunk and were all very merry, the old King put a riddle to the Waiting-woman. 'What does a person deserve who deceives his master?' telling the whole story, and ending by asking, 'What doom does he deserve?'

The false bride answered, 'No better than this. He must be put stark naked into a barrel stuck with nails, and be dragged along by two white horses from street to street till he is dead.'

'That is your own doom,' said the King, 'and the judgment shall be carried out.'

When the sentence was fulfilled, the young Prince married his true bride, and they ruled their kingdom together in peace and happiness.

The Four Clever Brothers

THERE was once a poor man who had four sons, and when they were grown up, he said to them : 'Dear children, you must go out into the world now, for I have nothing to give you. You must each learn a trade and make your own way in the world.'

So the four Brothers took their sticks in their hands, bid their father good-bye, and passed out of the town gate.

When they had walked some distance, they came to four cross roads, which led into four different districts. Then the eldest one said : 'We must part here, but this day four years, we will meet here again, having in the meantime done our best to make our fortunes.'

Then each one went his own way. The eldest met an old man, who asked him where he came from, and what he was going to do.

' I want to learn a trade,' he answered.

Then the Man said : ' Come with me and learn to be a Thief.'

' No,' answered he, ' that is no longer considered an honest trade ; and the end of that song would be that I should swing as the clapper in a bell.'

' Oh,' said the Man, ' you need not be afraid of the gallows. I will only teach you how to take things no one else wants, or knows how to get hold of, and where no one can find you out.'

So he allowed himself to be persuaded, and under the Man's instructions he became such an expert thief that nothing was safe from him which he had once made up his mind to have.

The second Brother met a Man who put the same question to him, as to what he was going to do in the world.

So the four Brothers took their sticks in their hands, bade their Father
good-bye, and passed out of the town gate.

' I don't know yet,' he answered.

' Then come with me and be a Star-gazer. It is the grandest thing in the world, nothing is hidden from you.'

He was pleased with the idea, and became such a clever Star-gazer, that when he had learnt everything and wanted to go away, his master gave him a telescope, and said—

' With this you can see everything that happens in the sky and on earth, and nothing can remain hidden from you.'

The third Brother was taken in hand by a Huntsman, who taught him everything connected with sport so well, that he became a first-rate Huntsman.

On his departure his master presented him with a gun, and said : ' This gun will never miss : whatever you aim at you will hit without fail.'

The youngest Brother also met a Man who asked him what he was going to do.

' Wouldn't you like to be a Tailor ? ' he asked.

' I don't know about that,' said the young man. ' I don't much fancy sitting cross-legged from morning till night, and everlastingly pulling a needle in and out, and pushing a flat iron.'

' Dear, dear ! ' said the Man, ' what are you talking about ? If you come to me you will learn quite a different sort of tailoring. It is a most pleasant and agreeable trade, not to say most honourable.'

So he allowed himself to be talked over, and went with the Man, who taught him his trade thoroughly.

On his departure, he gave him a needle, and said : ' With this needle you will be able to stitch anything together, be it as soft as an egg, or as hard as steel ; and it will become like a whole piece of stuff with no seam visible.'

When the four years, which the Brothers had agreed upon, had passed, they met at the cross-roads. They embraced one another and hurried home to their Father.

' Well ! ' said he, quite pleased to see them, ' has the wind wafted you back to me again ? '

They told him all that had happened to them, and that each had mastered a trade. They were sitting in front of the house under a big tree, and their Father said—

' Now, I will put you to the test, and see what you can do.'

Then he looked up and said to his second son—

' There is a chaffinch's nest in the topmost branch of this tree ; tell me how many eggs there are in it ? '

The Star-gazer took his glass and said : ' There are five.'

His Father said to the eldest : ' Bring the eggs down without disturbing the bird sitting on them.'

The cunning Thief climbed up and took the five eggs from under the bird so cleverly that it never noticed they were gone, and he gave them to his Father. His Father took them, and put them one on each corner of the table, and one in the middle, and said to the Sportsman—

' You must shoot the five eggs through the middle at one shot.'

The Sportsman levelled his gun, and divided each egg in half at one shot, as his Father desired. He certainly must have had some of the powder which shoots round the corner.

' Now it is your turn,' said his Father to the fourth son. ' You will sew the eggs together again, the shells and the young birds inside them ; and you will do it in such a manner that they will be none the worse for the shot.'

The Tailor produced his needle, and stitched away as his Father ordered. When he had finished, the Thief had to climb up the tree again, and put the eggs back under the bird without her noticing it. The bird spread herself over the eggs, and a few days later the fledglings crept out of the shell, and they all had a red line round their throats where the Tailor had sewn them together.

' Yes,' said the old man to his sons ; ' I can certainly praise your skill. You have learnt something worth knowing, and made the most of your time. I don't know which of you to give the palm to. I only hope you may soon have a chance of showing your skill so that it may be settled.'

65

Not long after this there was a great alarm raised in the country : the King's only daughter had been carried off by a Dragon. The King sorrowed for her day and night, and proclaimed that whoever brought her back should marry her.

The four Brothers said to one another : ' This would be an opportunity for us to prove what we can do.' And they decided to go out together to deliver the Princess.

' I shall soon know where she is,' said the Star-gazer, as he looked through his telescope ; and then he said—

' I see her already. She is a long way from here, she is sitting on a rock in the middle of the sea, and the Dragon is near, watching her.'

Then he went to the King and asked for a ship for himself and his Brothers to cross the sea in search of the rock.

They found the Princess still on the rock, but the Dragon was asleep with his head on her lap.

The Sportsman said : ' I dare not shoot. I should kill the beautiful maiden.'

' Then I will try my luck,' said the Thief, and he stole her away from beneath the Dragon. He did it so gently and skilfully, that the monster never discovered it, but went snoring on.

Full of joy, they hurried away with her to the ship, and steered for the open sea. But the Dragon on waking had missed the Princess, and now came after them through the air, foaming with rage.

Just as he was hovering over the ship and about to drop on them, the Sportsman took aim with his gun and shot him through the heart. The monster fell down dead, but he was so huge, that in falling, he dragged the whole ship down with him. They managed to seize a few boards, on which they kept themselves afloat.

They were now in great straits, but the Tailor, not to be outdone, produced his wonderful needle, and put some great stitches into the boards, seated himself on them, and collected all the floating bits of the ship. Then he stitched them all

The King's only daughter had been carried off by a Dragon.

They found the Princess still on the rock, but the Dragon was asleep
with his head on her lap.

together so cleverly, that in a very short time the ship was seaworthy again, and they sailed happily home.

The King was overjoyed when he saw his daughter again, and he said to the four Brothers : ' One of you shall marry her, but which one, you must decide among yourselves.'

An excited discussion then took place among them, for each one made a claim.

The Star-gazer said : ' Had I not discovered the Princess, all your arts would have been in vain, therefore she is mine ! '

The Thief said : ' What would have been the good of discovering her if I had not taken her from under the Dragon ? So she is mine.'

The Sportsman said : ' You, as well as the Princess, would have been destroyed by the monster if my shot had not hit him. So she is mine.'

The Tailor said : ' And if I had not sewn the ship together with my skill, you would all have been drowned miserably. Therefore she is mine.'

The King said : ' Each of you has an equal right ; but, as you can't all have her, none of you shall have her. I will give every one of you half a kingdom as a reward.'

The Brothers were quite satisfied with this decision, and they said : ' It is better so than that we should quarrel over it.'

So each of them received half a kingdom, and they lived happily with their Father for the rest of their days.

The Frog Prince

IN the olden time, when wishing was some good, there lived a King whose daughters were all beautiful, but the youngest was so lovely that even the sun, that looked on many things, could not but marvel when he shone upon her face.

Near the King's palace there was a large dark forest, and in the forest, under an old lime-tree, was a well. When the day was very hot the Princess used to go into the forest and sit upon the edge of this cool well; and when she was tired of doing nothing she would play with a golden ball, throwing it up in the air and catching it again, and this was her favourite game. Now on one occasion it so happened that the ball did not fall back into her hand stretched up to catch it, but dropped to the ground and rolled straight into the well. The Princess followed it with her eyes, but it disappeared, for the well was so very deep that it was quite impossible to see the bottom. Then she began to cry bitterly, and nothing would comfort her.

As she was lamenting in this manner, some one called out to her, 'What is the matter, Princess? Your lamentations would move the heart of a stone.'

She looked round towards the spot whence the voice came, and saw a Frog stretching its broad, ugly face out of the water.

'Oh, it's you, is it, old splasher? I am crying for my golden ball which has fallen into the water.'

'Be quiet then, and stop crying,' answered the Frog. 'I know what to do; but what will you give me if I get you back your plaything?'

'Whatever you like, you dear old Frog,' she said. 'My

clothes, my pearls and diamonds, or even the golden crown upon my head.'

The Frog answered, ' I care neither for your clothes, your pearls and diamonds, nor even your golden crown ; but if you will be fond of me, and let me be your playmate, sit by you at table, eat out of your plate, drink out of your cup, and sleep in your little bed—if you will promise to do all this, I will go down and fetch your ball.'

' I will promise anything you like to ask, if only you will get me back my ball.'

She thought, ' What is the silly old Frog chattering about ? He lives in the well, croaking with his mates, and he can't be the companion of a human being.'

As soon as the Frog received her promise, he ducked his head under the water and disappeared. After a little while, back he came with the ball in his mouth, and threw it on to the grass beside her.

The Princess was full of joy when she saw her pretty toy again, picked it up, and ran off with it.

' Wait, wait,' cried the Frog. ' Take me with you ; I can't run as fast as you can.'

But what was the good of his crying ' Croak, croak,' as loud as he could ? She did not listen to him, but hurried home, and forgot all about the poor Frog ; and he had to go back to his well.

The next day, as she was sitting at dinner with the King and all the courtiers, eating out of her golden plate, something came flopping up the stairs, flip, flap, flip, flap. When it reached the top it knocked at the door, and cried : ' Youngest daughter of the King, you must let me in.' She ran to see who it was. When she opened the door and saw the Frog she shut it again very quickly, and went back to the table, for she was very much frightened.

The King saw that her heart was beating very fast, and he said : ' My child, what is the matter ? Is there a giant at the door wanting to take you away ? '

'Oh no!' she said: 'it's not a giant, but a hideous Frog.'

'What does the Frog want with you?'

'Oh, father dear, last night, when I was playing by the well in the forest, my golden ball fell into the water. And I cried, and the Frog got it out for me; and then, because he insisted on it, I promised that he should be my playmate. But I never thought that he would come out of the water, but there he is, and he wants to come in to me.'

He knocked at the door for the second time, and sang—

> 'Youngest daughter of the King,
> Take me up, I sing;
> Know'st thou not what yesterday
> Thou to me didst say
> By the well in forest dell.
> Youngest daughter of the King,
> Take me up, I sing.'

Then said the King, 'What you have promised you must perform. Go and open the door for him.'

So she opened the door, and the Frog shuffled in, keeping close to her feet, till he reached her chair. Then he cried, 'Lift me up beside you.' She hesitated, till the King ordered her to do it. When the Frog was put on the chair, he demanded to be placed upon the table, and then he said, 'Push your golden plate nearer that we may eat together.' She did as he asked her, but very unwillingly, as could easily be seen. The Frog made a good dinner, but the Princess could not swallow a morsel. At last he said, 'I have eaten enough, and I am tired, carry me into your bedroom and arrange your silken bed, that we may go to sleep.'

The Princess began to cry, for she was afraid of the clammy Frog, which she did not dare to touch, and which was now to sleep in her pretty little silken bed. But the King grew very angry, and said, 'You must not despise any one who has helped you in your need.'

So she seized him with two fingers, and carried him upstairs, where she put him in a corner of her room. When she got into

So she seized him with two fingers, and carried him upstairs.

bed, he crept up to her, and said, 'I am tired, and I want to go to sleep as well as you. Lift me up, or I will tell your father.'

She was very angry, picked him up, and threw him with all her might against the wall, saying, 'You may rest there as well as you can, you hideous Frog.' But when he fell to the ground, he was no longer a hideous Frog, but a handsome Prince with beautiful friendly eyes.

And at her father's wish he became her beloved companion and husband. He told her that he had been bewitched by a wicked fairy, and nobody could have released him from the spells but she herself.

Next morning, when the sun rose, a coach drove up drawn by eight milk-white horses, with white ostrich plumes on their heads, and golden harness. Behind stood faithful Henry, the Prince's body-servant. The faithful fellow had been so distressed when his master was changed into a Frog, that he had caused three iron bands to be placed round his heart, lest it should break from grief and pain.

The coach had come to carry the young pair back into the Prince's own kingdom. The faithful Henry helped both of them into the coach and mounted again behind, delighted at his master's deliverance.

They had only gone a little way when the Prince heard a cracking behind him, as if something were breaking. He turned round, and cried—

> ' " Henry, the coach is giving way ! "
> " No, Sir, the coach is safe, I say,
> A band from my heart has fall'n in twain,
> For long I suffered woe and pain,
> While you a frog within a well
> Enchanted were by witch's spell ! " '

Once more he heard the same snapping and cracking, and then again. The Prince thought it must be some part of the carriage giving way, but it was only the bands round faithful Henry's heart which were snapping, because of his great joy at his master's deliverance and happiness.

74

Rumpelstiltskin

THERE was once a Miller who was very poor, but he had a beautiful daughter. Now, it fell out that he had occasion to speak with the King, and, in order to give himself an air of importance, he said : ' I have a daughter who can spin gold out of straw.'

The King said to the Miller : ' That is an art in which I am much interested. If your daughter is as skilful as you say she is, bring her to my castle to-morrow, and I will put her to the test.'

Accordingly, when the girl was brought to the castle, the King conducted her to a chamber which was quite full of straw, gave her a spinning-wheel and winder, and said, ' Now, set to work, and if between to-night and to-morrow at dawn you have not spun this straw into gold you must die.' Thereupon he carefully locked the door of the chamber, and she remained alone.

There sat the unfortunate Miller's daughter, and for the life of her did not know what to do. She had not the least idea how to spin straw into gold, and she became more and more distressed, until at last she began to weep. Then all at once the door sprang open, and in stepped a little Mannikin, who said : ' Good evening, Mistress Miller, what are you weeping so for ? '

' Alas ! ' answered the Maiden, ' I 've got to spin gold out of straw, and don't know how to do it.'

Then the Mannikin said, ' What will you give me if I spin it for you ? '

' My necklace,' said the Maid.

The little Man took the necklace, sat down before the

spinning-wheel, and whir—whir—whir, in a trice the reel was full.

Then he fixed another reel, and whir—whir—whir, thrice round, and that too was full; and so it went on until morning, when all the straw was spun and all the reels were full of gold.

Immediately at sunrise the King came, and when he saw the gold he was astonished and much pleased, but his mind became only the more avaricious. So he had the Miller's daughter taken to another chamber, larger than the former one, and full of straw, and he ordered her to spin it also in one night, as she valued her life.

The Maiden was at her wit's end, and began to weep. Then again the door sprang open, and the little Mannikin appeared, and said, 'What will you give me if I spin the straw into gold for you?'

'The ring off my finger,' answered the Maiden.

The little man took the ring, began to whir again at the wheel, and had by morning spun all the straw into gold.

Then all at once the door sprang open, and in stepped a little Mannikin.

The King was delighted at sight of the masses of gold, but was not even yet satisfied. So he had the Miller's daughter taken to a still larger chamber, full of straw, and said, 'This must you to-night spin into gold, but if you succeed you shall become my Queen.' 'Even if she is only a Miller's daughter,' thought he, 'I shan't find a richer woman in the whole world.'

76

When the girl was alone the little Man came again, and said for the third time, 'What will you give me if I spin the straw for you this time?'

'I have nothing more that I can give,' answered the girl.

'Well, promise me your first child if you become Queen.'

'Who knows what may happen,' thought the Miller's daughter; but she did not see any other way of getting out of the difficulty, so she promised the little Man what he demanded, and in return he spun the straw into gold once more.

When the King came in the morning, and found everything as he had wished, he celebrated his marriage with her, and the Miller's daughter became Queen.

About a year afterwards a beautiful child was born, but the Queen had forgotten all about the little Man. However, he suddenly entered her chamber, and said, 'Now, give me what you promised.'

The Queen was terrified, and offered the little Man all the wealth of the kingdom if he would let her keep the child. But the Mannikin said, 'No; I would rather have some living thing than all the treasures of the world.' Then the Queen began to moan and weep to such an extent that the little Man felt sorry for her. 'I will give you three days,' said he, 'and if within that time you discover my name you shall keep the child.'

Then during the night the Queen called to mind all the names that she had ever heard, and sent a messenger all over the country to inquire far and wide what other names there were. When the little Man came on the next day, she began with Caspar, Melchoir, Balzer, and mentioned all the names which she knew, one after the other; but at every one the little Man said : 'No; that 's not my name.'

The second day she had inquiries made all round the neighbourhood for the names of people living there, and suggested to the little Man all the most unusual and strange names.

'Perhaps your name is Cowribs, Spindleshanks, or Spiderlegs?'

But he answered every time, 'No; that's not my name.'

On the third day the messenger came back and said: 'I haven't been able to find any new names, but as I came round the corner of a wood on a lofty mountain, where the Fox says good-night to the Hare, I saw a little house, and in front of the house a fire was burning; and around the fire an indescribably ridiculous little man was leaping, hopping on one leg, and singing:

"To-day I bake; to-morrow I brew my beer;
The next day I will bring the Queen's child here.
Ah! lucky 'tis that not a soul doth know
That Rumpelstiltskin is my name, ho! ho!"'

Then you can imagine how delighted the Queen was when she heard the name, and when presently afterwards the little Man came in and asked, 'Now, your Majesty, what is my name?' at first she asked:

'Is your name Tom?'

'No.'

'Is it Dick?'

'No.'

'Is it, by chance, Rumpelstiltskin?'

'The devil told you that! The devil told you that!' shrieked the little Man; and in his rage stamped his right foot into the ground so deep that he sank up to his waist.

Then, in his passion, he seized his left leg with both hands, and tore himself asunder in the middle.

Round the fire an indescribably ridiculous little man was leaping, hopping
on one leg, and singing.

Jorinda and Joringel

THERE was once an old castle in the middle of a vast thick wood; in it there lived an old woman quite alone, and she was a witch. By day she made herself into a cat or a screech-owl, but regularly at night she became a human being again. In this way she was able to decoy wild beasts and birds, which she would kill, and boil or roast. If any man came within a hundred paces of the castle, he was forced to stand still and could not move from the place till she gave the word of release; but if an innocent maiden came within the circle she changed her into a bird, and shut her up in a cage which she carried into a room in the castle. She must have had seven thousand cages of this kind, containing pretty birds.

Now, there was once a maiden called Jorinda who was more beautiful than all other maidens. She had promised to marry a very handsome youth named Joringel, and it was in the days of their courtship, when they took the greatest joy in being alone together, that one day they wandered out into the forest. 'Take care,' said Joringel; 'do not let us go too near the castle.'

It was a lovely evening. The sunshine glanced between the tree-trunks of the dark green-wood, while the turtle-doves sang plaintively in the old beech-trees. Yet Jorinda sat down in the sunshine, and could not help weeping and bewailing, while Joringel, too, soon became just as mournful. They both felt as miserable as if they had been going to die. Gazing round them, they found they had lost their way, and did not know how they should find the path home. Half the sun still appeared above the mountain; half had sunk

. . . Or a screech-owl.

below. Joringel peered into the bushes and saw the old walls of the castle quite close to them ; he was terror-struck, and became pale as death. Jorinda was singing :

> 'My birdie with its ring so red
>   Sings sorrow, sorrow, sorrow ;
> My love will mourn when I am dead,
>   To-morrow, morrow, mor—— jug, jug.'

Joringel looked at her, but she was changed into a nightingale who sang ' Jug, jug.'

A screech-owl with glowing eyes flew three times round her, and cried three times ' Shu hu-hu.' Joringel could not stir ; he stood like a stone without being able to speak, or cry, or move hand or foot. The sun had now set ; the owl flew into a bush, out of which appeared almost at the same moment a crooked old woman, skinny and yellow ; she had big, red eyes and a crooked nose whose tip reached her chin. She mumbled something, caught the nightingale, and carried it away in her hand. Joringel could not say a word nor move from the spot, and the nightingale was gone. At last the old woman came back, and said in a droning voice : ' Greeting to thee, Zachiel ! When the moon shines upon the cage, unloose the captive, Zachiel ! '

Then Joringel was free. He fell on his knees before the witch, and implored her to give back his Jorinda ; but she said he should never have her again, and went away. He pleaded, he wept, he lamented, but all in vain. ' Alas ! what is to become of me ? ' said Joringel. At last he went away, and arrived at a strange village, where he spent a long time as a shepherd. He often wandered round about the castle, but did not go too near it. At last he dreamt one night that he found a blood-red flower, in the midst of which was a beautiful large pearl. He plucked the flower, and took it to the castle. Whatever he touched with it was made free of enchantment. He dreamt, too, that by this means he had found his Jorinda again. In the morning when he awoke he

At last the old woman came back, and said in a droning voice: 'Greeting to thee, Zachiel!'

began to search over hill and dale, in the hope of finding a
flower like this; he searched till the ninth day, when he found
the flower early in the morning. In the middle was a big
dewdrop, as big as the finest pearl. This flower he carried
day and night, till he reached the castle. He was not held
fast as before when he came within the hundred paces of the
castle, but walked straight up to the door.

Joringel was filled with joy; he touched the door with the
flower, and it flew open. He went in through the court, and
listened for the sound of birds. He went on, and found the
hall, where the witch was feeding the birds in the seven
thousand cages. When she saw Joringel she was angry,
very angry—scolded, and spat poison and gall at him. He
paid no attention to her, but turned away and searched among
the bird-cages. Yes, but there were many hundred nightin-
gales; how was he to find his Jorinda?

While he was looking about in this way he noticed that the
old woman was secretly removing a cage with a bird inside,
and was making for the door. He sprang swiftly towards her,
touched the cage and the witch with the flower, and then
she no longer had power to exercise her spells. Jorinda stood
there, as beautiful as before, and threw her arms round
Joringel's neck. After that he changed all the other birds
back into maidens again, and went home with Jorinda, and
they lived long and happily together.

The Wolf and the Seven Kids

THERE was once an old Nanny-goat who had seven Kids, and she was just as fond of them as a mother of her children. One day she was going into the woods to fetch some food for them, so she called them all up to her, and said—

' My dear children, I am going out into the woods. Beware of the Wolf! If once he gets into the house, he will eat you up, skin, and hair, and all. The rascal often disguises himself, but you will know him by his rough voice and his black feet.'

The Kids said, ' Oh, we will be very careful, dear mother. You may be quite happy about us.'

Bleating tenderly, the old Goat went off to her work. Before long, some one knocked at the door, and cried—

' Open the door, dear children ' Your mother has come back and brought something for each of you.'

But the Kids knew quite well by the voice that it was the Wolf.

' We won't open the door,' they cried. ' You are not our mother. She has a soft gentle voice; but yours is rough, and we are quite sure that you are the Wolf.'

So he went away to a shop and bought a lump of chalk, which he ate, and it made his voice quite soft. He went back, knocked at the door again, and cried—

' Open the door, dear children. Your mother has come back and brought something for each of you.'

But the Wolf had put one of his paws on the window sill, where the Kids saw it, and cried—

' We won't open the door. Our mother has not got a black foot as you have; you are the Wolf.'

Then the Wolf ran to a Baker, and said, 'I have bruised my foot; please put some dough on it.' And when the Baker had put some dough on his foot, he ran to the Miller and said, 'Strew some flour on my foot.'

The Miller thought, 'The old Wolf is going to take somebody in,' and refused.

But the Wolf said, 'If you don't do it, I will eat you up.'

So the Miller was frightened, and whitened his paws. People are like that, you know.

Now the wretch went for the third time to the door, and knocked, and said—

'Open the door, children. Your dear mother has come home, and has brought something for each of you out of the wood.'

The Kids cried, 'Show us your feet first, that we may be sure you are our mother.'

He put his paws on the window sill, and when they saw that they were white, they believed all he said, and opened the door.

Alas! It was the Wolf who walked in. They were terrified, and tried to hide themselves. One ran under the table, the second jumped into bed, the third into the oven, the fourth ran into the kitchen, the fifth got into the cupboard, the sixth into the wash-tub, and the seventh hid in the tall clock-case. But the Wolf found them all but one, and made short work of them. He swallowed one after the other, except the youngest one in the clock-case, whom he did not find. When he had satisfied his appetite, he took himself off, and lay down in a meadow outside, where he soon fell asleep.

Not long after the old Nanny-goat came back from the woods. Oh! what a terrible sight met her eyes! The house door was wide open, table, chairs, and benches were overturned, the washing bowl was smashed to atoms, the covers and pillows torn from the bed. She searched all over the house for her children, but nowhere were they to be found. She called them by name, one by one, but no one answered.

At last, when she came to the youngest, a tiny voice cried:

'I am here, dear mother, hidden in the clock-case.'

She brought him out, and he told her that the Wolf had come and devoured all the others.

You may imagine how she wept over her children.

At last, in her grief, she went out, and the youngest Kid ran by her side. When they went into the meadow, there lay the Wolf under a tree, making the branches shake with his snores. They examined him from every side, and they could plainly see movements within his distended body.

'Ah, heavens!' thought the Goat, 'is it possible that my poor children whom he ate for his supper, should be still alive?'

She sent the Kid running to the house to fetch scissors, needles, and thread. Then she cut a hole in the monster's side, and, hardly had she begun, when a Kid popped out its head, and as soon as the hole was big enough, all six jumped out, one after the other, all alive, and without having suffered the least injury, for, in his greed, the monster had swallowed them whole. You may imagine the mother's joy. She hugged them, and skipped about like a tailor on his wedding day. At last she said:

'Go and fetch some big stones, children, and we will fill up the brute's body while he is asleep.'

Then the seven Kids brought a lot of stones, as fast as they could carry them, and stuffed the Wolf with them till he could hold no more. The old mother quickly sewed him up, without his having noticed anything, or even moved.

At last, when the Wolf had had his sleep out, he got up, and, as the stones made him feel very thirsty, he wanted to go to a spring to drink. But as soon as he moved the stones began to roll about and rattle inside him. Then he cried—

'What's the rumbling and tumbling
That sets my stomach grumbling?
I thought 'twas six Kids, flesh and bones,
Now find it's nought but rolling stones.'

87

When he reached the spring, and stooped over the water to drink, the heavy stones dragged him down, and he was drowned miserably.

When the seven Kids saw what had happened, they came running up, and cried aloud—'The Wolf is dead, the Wolf is dead!' and they and their mother capered and danced round the spring in their joy.

The seven Kids and their mother capered and danced
round the spring in their joy.

Hansel and Grethel

CLOSE to a large forest there lived a Woodcutter with his Wife and his two children. The boy was called Hansel, and the girl Grethel. They were always very poor, and had very little to live on; and at one time, when there was famine in the land, he could no longer procure daily bread.

One night he lay in bed worrying over his troubles, and he sighed and said to his Wife: 'What is to become of us? How are we to feed our poor children when we have nothing for ourselves?'

'I'll tell you what, Husband,' answered the Woman, 'to-morrow morning we will take the children out quite early into the thickest part of the forest. We will light a fire, and give each of them a piece of bread; then we will go to our work and leave them alone. They won't be able to find their way back, and so we shall be rid of them.'

'Nay, Wife,' said the Man; 'we won't do that. I could never find it in my heart to leave my children alone in the forest; the wild animals would soon tear them to pieces.'

'What a fool you are!' she said. 'Then we must all four die of hunger. You may as well plane the boards for our coffins at once.'

She gave him no peace till he consented. 'But I grieve over the poor children all the same,' said the Man.

The two children could not go to sleep for hunger either, and they heard what their Stepmother said to their Father.

Grethel wept bitterly, and said: 'All is over with us now!'

'Be quiet, Grethel!' said Hansel. 'Don't cry; I will find some way out of it.'

90

When the old people had gone to sleep, he got up, put on
his little coat, opened the door, and slipped out. The moon
was shining brightly, and the white pebbles round the house
shone like newly-minted coins. Hansel stooped down and
put as many into his pockets as they would hold.

Then he went back to Grethel, and said : ' Take comfort,
little sister, and go to sleep. God won't forsake us.' And
then he went to bed again.

When the day broke, before the sun had risen, the Woman
came and said : ' Get up, you lazybones ; we are going into
the forest to fetch wood.'

Then she gave them each a piece of bread, and said :
' Here is something for your dinner, but mind you don't eat
it before, for you 'll get no more.'

Grethel put the bread under her apron, for Hansel had the
stones in his pockets. Then they all started for the forest.

When they had gone a little way, Hansel stopped and looked
back at the cottage, and he did the same thing again and again.

His Father said : ' Hansel, what are you stopping to look
back at ? Take care, and put your best foot foremost.'

' O Father ! ' said Hansel, ' I am looking at my white
cat, it is sitting on the roof, wanting to say good-bye to me.'

' Little fool ! that 's no cat, it 's the morning sun shining
on the chimney.'

But Hansel had not been looking at the cat, he had been
dropping a pebble on to the ground each time he stopped.
When they reached the middle of the forest, their Father said:

' Now, children, pick up some wood, I want to make a fire
to warm you.'

Hansel and Grethel gathered the twigs together and soon
made a huge pile. Then the pile was lighted, and when it
blazed up, the Woman said : ' Now lie down by the fire and
rest yourselves while we go and cut wood ; when we have
finished we will come back to fetch you.'

Hansel and Grethel sat by the fire, and when dinner-time
came they each ate their little bit of bread, and they thought

Hansel picked up the glittering white pebbles and filled his pockets with them.

their Father was quite near because they could hear the sound of an axe. It was no axe, however, but a branch which the Man had tied to a dead tree, and which blew backwards and forwards against it. They sat there such a long time that they got tired, their eyes began to close, and they were soon fast asleep.

When they woke it was dark night. Grethel began to cry : ' How shall we ever get out of the wood ! '

But Hansel comforted her, and said : ' Wait a little till the moon rises, then we will soon find our way.'

When the full moon rose, Hansel took his little sister's hand, and they walked on, guided by the pebbles, which glittered like newly-coined money. They walked the whole night, and at daybreak they found themselves back at their Father's cottage.

They knocked at the door, and when the Woman opened it and saw Hansel and Grethel, she said : ' You bad children, why did you sleep so long in the wood ? We thought you did not mean to come back any more.'

But their Father was delighted, for it had gone to his heart to leave them behind alone.

Not long after they were again in great destitution, and the children heard the Woman at night in bed say to their Father : ' We have eaten up everything again but half a loaf, and then we are at the end of everything. The children must go away ; we will take them further into the forest so that they won't be able to find their way back. There is nothing else to be done.'

The Man took it much to heart, and said : ' We had better share our last crust with the children.'

But the Woman would not listen to a word he said, she only scolded and reproached him. Any one who once says A must also say B, and as he had given in the first time, he had to do so the second also. The children were again wide awake and heard what was said.

When the old people went to sleep Hansel again got up,

meaning to go out and get some more pebbles, but the Woman had locked the door and he couldn't get out. But he consoled his little sister, and said :

'Don't cry, Grethel ; go to sleep. God will help us.'

In the early morning the Woman made the children get up, and gave them each a piece of bread, but it was smaller than the last. On the way to the forest Hansel crumbled it up in his pocket, and stopped every now and then to throw a crumb on to the ground.

'Hansel, what are you stopping to look about you for ? ' asked his Father.

'I am looking at my dove which is sitting on the roof and wants to say good-bye to me,' answered Hansel.

'Little fool ! ' said the Woman, 'that is no dove, it is the morning sun shining on the chimney.'

Nevertheless, Hansel strewed the crumbs from time to time on the ground. The Woman led the children far into the forest where they had never been in their lives before. Again they made a big fire, and the Woman said :

'Stay where you are, children, and when you are tired you may go to sleep for a while. We are going further on to cut wood, and in the evening when we have finished we will come back and fetch you.'

At dinner-time Grethel shared her bread with Hansel, for he had crumbled his up on the road. Then they went to sleep, and the evening passed, but no one came to fetch the poor children.

It was quite dark when they woke up, and Hansel cheered his little sister, and said : 'Wait a bit, Grethel, till the moon rises, then we can see the bread-crumbs which I scattered to show us the way home.'

When the moon rose they started, but they found no bread-crumbs, for all the thousands of birds in the forest had pecked them up and eaten them.

Hansel said to Grethel : ' We shall soon find the way.'

But they could not find it. They walked the whole night,

94

and all the next day from morning till night, but they could not get out of the wood.

They were very hungry, for they had nothing to eat but a few berries which they found. They were so tired that their legs would not carry them any further, and they lay down under a tree and went to sleep.

When they woke in the morning, it was the third day since they had left their Father's cottage. They started to walk again, but they only got deeper and deeper into the wood, and if no help came they must perish.

At midday they saw a beautiful snow-white bird sitting on a tree. It sang so beautifully that they stood still to listen to it. When it stopped, it fluttered its wings and flew round them. They followed it till they came to a little cottage, on the roof of which it settled itself.

When they got quite near, they saw that the little house was made of bread, and it was roofed with cake; the windows were transparent sugar.

'This will be something for us,' said Hansel. 'We will have a good meal. I will have a piece of the roof, Grethel, and you can have a bit of the window, it will be nice and sweet.'

Hansel stretched up and broke off a piece of the roof to try what it was like. Grethel went to the window and nibbled at that. A gentle voice called out from within:

'Nibbling, nibbling like a mouse,
Who's nibbling at my little house?'

The children answered:

'The wind, the wind doth blow
From heaven to earth below,'

and went on eating without disturbing themselves. Hansel, who found the roof very good, broke off a large piece for himself; and Grethel pushed a whole round pane out of the window, and sat down on the ground to enjoy it.

95

All at once the door opened and an old, old Woman, supporting herself on a crutch, came hobbling out. Hansel and Grethel were so frightened, that they dropped what they held in their hands.

But the old Woman only shook her head, and said : ' Ah, dear children, who brought you here ? Come in and stay with me ; you will come to no harm.'

She took them by the hand and led them into the little house. A nice dinner was set before them, pancakes and sugar, milk, apples, and nuts. After this she showed them two little white beds into which they crept, and felt as if they were in Heaven.

Although the old Woman appeared to be so friendly, she was really a wicked old Witch who was on the watch for children, and she had built the bread house on purpose to lure them to her. Whenever she could get a child into her clutches she cooked it and ate it, and considered it a grand feast. Witches have red eyes, and can't see very far, but they have keen scent like animals, and can perceive the approach of human beings.

When Hansel and Grethel came near her, she laughed wickedly to herself, and said scornfully : ' Now I have them, they shan't escape me.'

She got up early in the morning, before the children were awake, and when she saw them sleeping, with their beautiful rosy cheeks, she murmured to herself : ' They will be dainty morsels.'

She seized Hansel with her bony hand and carried him off to a little stable, where she shut him up with a barred door ; he might shriek as loud as he liked, she took no notice of him. Then she went to Grethel and shook her till she woke, and cried :

' Get up, little lazy-bones, fetch some water and cook something nice for your brother ; he is in the stable, and has to be fattened. When he is nice and fat, I will eat him.'

Grethel began to cry bitterly, but it was no use, she had

96

All at once the door opened and an old, old Woman, supporting
herself on a crutch, came hobbling out.

to obey the Witch's orders. The best food was now cooked for poor Hansel, but Grethel only had the shells of cray-fish.

The old Woman hobbled to the stable every morning, and cried: 'Hansel, put your finger out for me to feel how fat you are.'

Hansel put out a knuckle-bone, and the old Woman, whose eyes were dim, could not see, and thought it was his finger, and she was much astonished that he did not get fat.

When four weeks had passed, and Hansel still kept thin, she became very impatient and would wait no longer.

'Now then, Grethel,' she cried, 'bustle along and fetch the water. Fat or thin, to-morrow I will kill Hansel and eat him.'

Oh, how his poor little sister grieved. As she carried the water, the tears streamed down her cheeks.

'Dear God, help us!' she cried. 'If only the wild animals in the forest had devoured us, we should, at least, have died together.'

'You may spare your lamentations; they will do you no good,' said the old Woman.

Early in the morning Grethel had to go out to fill the kettle with water, and then she had to kindle a fire and hang the kettle over it.

'We will bake first,' said the old Witch. 'I have heated the oven and kneaded the dough.'

She pushed poor Grethel towards the oven, and said: 'Creep in and see if it is properly heated, and then we will put the bread in.'

She meant, when Grethel had got in, to shut the door and roast her.

But Grethel saw her intention, and said: 'I don't know how to get in. How am I to manage it?'

'Stupid goose!' cried the Witch. 'The opening is big enough; you can see that I could get into it myself.'

She hobbled up, and stuck her head into the oven. But

98

Hansel put out a knuckle-bone, and the old Woman, whose eyes were
dim, could not see, and thought it was his finger, and she was
much astonished he did not get fat.

Grethel gave her a push which sent the Witch right in, and then she banged the door and bolted it.

'Oh! oh!' she began to howl horribly. But Grethel ran away and left the wicked Witch to perish miserably.

Grethel ran as fast as she could to the stable. She opened the door, and cried: 'Hansel, we are saved. The old Witch is dead.'

'Stupid goose!' cried the Witch. 'The opening is big enough; you can see that I could get into it myself.'

Hansel sprang out, like a bird out of a cage when the door is set open. How delighted they were. They fell upon each other's necks, and kissed each other, and danced about for joy.

As they had nothing more to fear, they went into the Witch's house, and they found chests in every corner full of pearls and precious stones.

100

'These are better than pebbles,' said Hansel, as he filled his pockets.

Grethel said : 'I must take something home with me too.' And she filled her apron.

'But now we must go,' said Hansel, 'so that we may get out of this enchanted wood.'

Before they had gone very far, they came to a great piece of water.

'We can't get across it,' said Hansel ; 'I see no stepping-stones and no bridge.'

'And there are no boats either,' answered Grethel. 'But there is a duck swimming, it will help us over if we ask it.'

So she cried—

> 'Little duck, that cries quack, quack,
> Here Grethel and here Hansel stand.
> Quickly, take us on your back,
> No path nor bridge is there at hand!'

The duck came swimming towards them, and Hansel got on its back, and told his sister to sit on his knee.

'No,' answered Grethel, 'it will be too heavy for the duck ; it must take us over one after the other.'

The good creature did this, and when they had got safely over and walked for a while, the wood seemed to grow more and more familiar to them, and at last they saw their Father's cottage in the distance. They began to run, and rushed inside, where they threw their arms round their Father's neck. The Man had not had a single happy moment since he had deserted his children in the wood, and in the meantime his Wife was dead.

Grethel shook her apron and scattered the pearls and precious stones all over the floor, and Hansel added handful after handful out of his pockets.

So all their troubles came to an end, and they lived together as happily as possible.

The Golden Goose

THERE was once a man who had three sons. The youngest of them was called Simpleton; he was scorned and despised by the others, and kept in the background.

The eldest son was going into the forest to cut wood, and before he started, his mother gave him a nice sweet cake and a bottle of wine to take with him, so that he might not suffer from hunger or thirst. In the wood he met a little, old, grey Man, who bade him good-day, and said, 'Give me a bit of the cake in your pocket, and let me have a drop of your wine. I am so hungry and thirsty.'

But the clever son said : 'If I give you my cake and wine, I shan't have enough for myself. Be off with you.'

He left the little Man standing there, and went on his way. But he had not been long at work, cutting down a tree, before he made a false stroke, and dug the axe into his own arm, and he was obliged to go home to have it bound up.

Now, this was no accident; it was brought about by the little grey Man.

The second son now had to go into the forest to cut wood, and, like the eldest, his mother gave him a sweet cake and a bottle of wine. In the same way the little grey Man met him, and asked for a piece of his cake and a drop of his wine. But the second son made the same sensible answer, 'If I give you any, I shall have the less for myself. Be off out of my way,' and he went on.

His punishment, however, was not long delayed. After a few blows at the tree, he hit his own leg, and had to be carried home.

Then Simpleton said, ' Let me go to cut the wood, father.'

But his father said, ' Your brothers have only come to harm by it; you had better leave it alone. You know nothing

There stands an old tree; cut it down, and you will find something at the roots.

about it.' But Simpleton begged so hard to be allowed to go that at last his father said, ' Well, off you go then. You will be wiser when you have hurt yourself.'

His mother gave him a cake which was only mixed with water and baked in the ashes, and a bottle of sour beer. When he reached the forest, like the others, he met the little grey

Man, who greeted him, and said, ' Give me a bit of your cake and a drop of your wine. I am so hungry and thirsty.'

Simpleton answered, ' I only have a cake baked in the ashes, and some sour beer ; but, if you like such fare, we will sit down and eat it together.'

So they sat down ; but when Simpleton pulled out his cake it was a sweet, nice cake, and his sour beer was turned into good wine. So they ate and drank, and the little Man said, ' As you have such a good heart, and are willing to share your goods, I

So now there were seven people running behind Simpleton and his Goose.

will give you good luck. There stands an old tree ; cut it down, and you will find something at the roots.'

So saying he disappeared.

Simpleton cut down the tree, and when it fell, lo, and behold ! a Goose was sitting among the roots, and its feathers were of pure gold. He picked it up, and taking it with him, went to an inn, where he meant to stay the night. The land-lord had three daughters, who saw the Goose, and were very curious as to what kind of bird it could be, and wanted to get one of its golden feathers.

The eldest thought, 'There will soon be some opportunity for me to pull out one of the feathers,' and when Simpleton went outside, she took hold of its wing to pluck out a feather; but her hand stuck fast, and she could not get away.

Soon after, the second sister came up, meaning also to pluck out one of the golden feathers; but she had hardly touched her sister when she found herself held fast.

Lastly, the third one came, with the same intention, but the others screamed out, 'Keep away! For goodness sake, keep away!'

But she, not knowing why she was to keep away, thought, 'Why should I not be there, if they are there?'

So she ran up, but as soon as she touched her sisters she had to stay hanging on to them, and they all had to pass the night like this.

In the morning, Simpleton took up the Goose under his arm, without noticing the three girls hanging on behind. They had to keep running behind, dodging his legs right and left.

In the middle of the fields they met the Parson, who, when he saw the procession, cried out: 'For shame, you bold girls! Why do you run after the lad like that? Do you call that proper behaviour?'

Then he took hold of the hand of the youngest girl to pull her away; but no sooner had he touched her than he felt himself held fast, and he, too, had to run behind.

Soon after the Sexton came up, and, seeing his master the Parson treading on the heels of the three girls, cried out in amazement, 'Hullo, your Reverence! Whither away so fast? Don't forget that we have a christening!'

So saying, he plucked the Parson by the sleeve, and soon found that he could not get away.

As this party of five, one behind the other, tramped on, two Peasants came along the road, carrying their hoes. The Parson called them, and asked them to set the Sexton and himself free. But as soon as ever they touched the Sexton they were held fast, so now there were seven people running behind Simpleton and his Goose.

By-and-by they reached a town, where a King ruled whose only daughter was so solemn that nothing and nobody could make her laugh. So the King had proclaimed that whoever could make her laugh should marry her.

When Simpleton heard this he took his Goose, with all his following, before her, and when she saw these seven people running, one behind another, she burst into fits of

laughter, and seemed as if she could never stop.

Thereupon Simpleton asked her in marriage. But the King did not like him for a son-in-law, and he made all sorts of conditions. First, he said Simpleton must bring him a man who could drink up a cellar full of wine.

Then Simpleton at once thought of the little grey Man

And so they followed up hill and down dale after Simpleton and his Goose.

who might be able to help him, and he went out to the forest to look for him. On the very spot where the tree that he had cut down had stood, he saw a man sitting with a very sad face. Simpleton asked him what was the matter, and he answered—

'I am so thirsty, and I can't quench my thirst. I hate cold water, and I have already emptied a cask of wine; but what is a drop like that on a burning stone?'

'Well, there I can help you,' said Simpleton. 'Come with me, and you shall soon have enough to drink and to spare.'

He led him to the King's cellar, and the Man set to upon the great casks, and he drank and drank till his sides ached, and by the end of the day the cellar was empty.

Then again Simpleton demanded his bride. But the King was annoyed that a wretched fellow called 'Simpleton' should have his daughter, and he made new conditions. He was now to find a man who could eat up a mountain of bread.

Simpleton did not reflect long, but went straight to the forest, and there in the self-same place sat a man tightening a strap round his body, and making a very miserable face. He said: 'I have eaten up a whole ovenful of rolls, but what is the good of that when any one is as hungry as I am. I am never satisfied. I have to tighten my belt every day if I am not to die of hunger.'

107

Simpleton was delighted, and said : ' Get up and come with me. You shall have enough to eat.'

And he took him to the Court, where the King had caused all the flour in the kingdom to be brought together, and a huge mountain of bread to be baked. The Man from the forest sat down before it and began to eat, and at the end of the day the whole mountain had disappeared.

Now, for the third time, Simpleton asked for his bride. But again the King tried to find an excuse, and demanded a ship which could sail on land as well as at sea.

' As soon as you sail up in it, you shall have my daughter,' he said.

Simpleton went straight to the forest, and there sat the little grey Man to whom he had given his cake. The little Man said : ' I have eaten and drunk for you, and now I will give you the ship, too. I do it all because you were merciful to me.'

Then he gave him the ship which could sail on land as well as at sea, and when the King saw it he could no longer withhold his daughter. The marriage was celebrated, and, at the King's death, the Simpleton inherited the kingdom, and lived long and happily with his wife.

The King could no longer withhold his daughter.

Ashenputtel

THE wife of a rich man fell ill, and when she felt that she was nearing her end, she called her only daughter to her bedside, and said:

'Dear child, continue devout and good, then God will always help you, and I will look down upon you from heaven, and watch over you.'

Thereupon she closed her eyes, and breathed her last.

The maiden went to her mother's grave every day and wept, and she continued to be devout and good. When the winter came, the snow spread a white covering on the grave, and when the sun of spring had unveiled it again, the husband took another wife. The new wife brought home with her two daughters, who were fair and beautiful to look upon, but base and black at heart.

Then began a sad time for the unfortunate step-child.

'Is this stupid goose to sit with us in the parlour?' they said.

'Whoever wants to eat bread must earn it; go and sit with the kitchenmaid.'

They took away her pretty clothes, and made her put on an old grey frock, and gave her wooden clogs.

'Just look at the proud Princess, how well she's dressed,' they laughed, as they led her to the kitchen. There, the girl was obliged to do hard work from morning till night, to get up at daybreak, carry water, light the fire, cook, and wash. Not content with that, the sisters inflicted on her every vexation they could think of; they made fun of her, and tossed the peas and lentils among the ashes, so that she had to sit down and pick them out again. In the evening, when she was worn out with work, she had no bed to go to, but had to lie on the hearth among the cinders. And because, on account of that, she always looked dusty and dirty, they called her Ashenputtel.

It happened one day that the Father had a mind to go to the Fair. So he asked both his step-daughters what he should bring home for them.

'Fine clothes,' said one.

'Pearls and jewels,' said the other.

'But you, Ashenputtel?' said he, 'what will you have?'

'Father, break off for me the first twig which brushes against your hat on your way home.'

Well, for his two step-daughters he brought beautiful clothes, pearls and jewels, and on his way home, as he was riding through a green copse, a hazel twig grazed against him and knocked his hat off. Then he broke off the branch and took it with him.

When he got home he gave his step-daughters what they had asked for, and to Ashenputtel he gave the twig from the hazel bush.

Ashenputtel thanked him, and went to her mother's grave and planted the twig upon it; she wept so much that her tears fell and watered it. And it took root and became a fine tree.

Ashenputtel went to the grave three times every day, wept and prayed, and every time a little white bird came and perched upon the tree, and when she uttered a wish, the little bird threw down to her what she had wished for.

Now it happened that the King proclaimed a festival, which was to last three days, and to which all the beautiful maidens in the country were invited, in order that his son might choose a bride.

When the two step-daughters heard that they were also to be present, they were in high spirits, called Ashenputtel, and said:

ASHENPUTTEL

'Brush our hair and clean our shoes, and fasten our buckles, for we are going to the feast at the King's palace.'

Ashenputtel obeyed, but wept, for she also would gladly have gone to the ball with them, and begged her step-mother to give her leave to go.

'You, Ashenputtel!' she said. 'Why, you are covered with dust and dirt. You go to the festival! Besides you have no clothes or shoes, and yet you want to go to the ball.'

As she, however, went on asking, her Step-mother said :

'Well, I have thrown a dishful of lentils into the cinders, if you have picked them all out in two hours you shall go with us.'

The girl went through the back door into the garden, and cried, 'Ye gentle doves, ye turtle doves, and all ye little birds under heaven, come and help me,

'The good into a dish to throw,
The bad into your crops can go.'

Then two white doves came in by the kitchen window, and were followed by the turtle doves, and finally all the little birds under heaven flocked in, chirping, and settled down among the ashes. And the doves gave a nod with their little heads, peck, peck, peck ; and then the rest began also, peck, peck, peck, and collected all the good beans into the dish. Scarcely had an hour passed before they had finished, and all flown out again.

Then the girl brought the dish to her Step-mother, and was delighted to think that now she would be able to go to the feast with them.

But she said, 'No, Ashenputtel, you have no clothes, and cannot dance ; you will only be laughed at.'

But when she began to cry, the Step-mother said :

'If you can pick out two whole dishes of lentils from the ashes in an hour, you shall go with us.'

And she thought, 'She will never be able to do that.'

When her Step-mother had thrown the dishes of lentils

111

among the ashes, the girl went out through the back door, and cried, ' Ye gentle doves, ye turtle doves, and all ye little birds under heaven, come and help me,

'The good into a dish to throw,
The bad into your crops can go.'

Then two white doves came in by the kitchen window, and were followed by the turtle doves, and all the other little birds under heaven, and in less than an hour the whole had been picked up, and they had all flown away.

Then the girl carried the dish to her Step-mother, and was delighted to think that she would now be able to go to the ball.

But she said, ' It 's not a bit of good. You can't go with us, for you 've got no clothes, and you can't dance. We should be quite ashamed of you.'

Thereupon she turned her back upon her, and hurried off with her two proud daughters.

As soon as every one had left the house, Ashenputtel went out to her mother's grave under the hazel-tree, and cried :

'Shiver and shake, dear little tree,
Gold and silver shower on me.'

Then the bird threw down to her a gold and silver robe, and a pair of slippers embroidered with silk and silver. With all speed she put on the robe and went to the feast. But her step-sisters and their mother did not recognise her, and supposed that she was some foreign Princess, so beautiful did she appear in her golden dress. They never gave a thought to Ashenputtel, but imagined that she was sitting at home in the dirt picking the lentils out of the cinders.

The Prince came up to the stranger, took her by the hand, and danced with her. In fact, he would not dance with any one else, and never left go of her hand. If any one came up to ask her to dance, he said, ' This is my partner.'

She danced until nightfall, and then wanted to go home ; but the Prince said, ' I will go with you and escort you.'

112

Ashenputtel goes to the ball.

For he wanted to see to whom the beautiful maiden belonged. But she slipped out of his way and sprang into the pigeon-house.

Then the Prince waited till her Father came, and told him that the unknown maiden had vanished into the pigeon-house.

The old man thought, 'Could it be Ashenputtel?' And he had an axe brought to him, so that he might break down the pigeon-house, but there was no one inside.

When they went home, there lay Ashenputtel in her dirty clothes among the cinders, and a dismal oil lamp was burning in the chimney corner. For Ashenputtel had quietly jumped down out of the pigeon-house and ran back to the hazel-tree. There she had taken off her beautiful clothes and laid them on the grave, and the bird had taken them away again. Then she had settled herself among the ashes on the hearth in her old grey frock.

On the second day, when the festival was renewed, and her parents and step-sisters had started forth again, Ashenputtel went to the hazel-tree, and said:

'Shiver and shake, dear little tree,
Gold and silver shower on me.'

Then the bird threw down a still more gorgeous robe than on the previous day. And when she appeared at the festival in this robe, every one was astounded by her beauty.

The King's son had waited till she came, and at once took her hand, and she danced with no one but him. When others came forward and invited her to dance, he said, 'This is my partner.'

At nightfall she wished to leave; but the Prince went after her, hoping to see into what house she went, but she sprang out into the garden behind the house. There stood a fine big tree on which the most delicious pears hung. She climbed up among the branches as nimbly as a squirrel, and the Prince could not make out what had become of her.

But he waited till her Father came, and then said to him,

'The unknown maiden has slipped away from me, and I think that she has jumped into the pear-tree.'

The Father thought, 'Can it be Ashenputtel?' And he had the axe brought to cut down the tree, but there was no one on it. When they went home and looked into the kitchen, there lay Ashenputtel among the cinders as usual; for she had jumped down on the other side of the tree, taken back the beautiful clothes to the bird on the hazel-tree, and put on her old grey frock.

On the third day, when her parents and sisters had started, Ashenputtel went again to her mother's grave, and said:

'Shiver and shake, dear little tree,
  Gold and silver shower on me.'

Then the bird threw down a dress which was so magnificent that no one had ever seen the like before, and the slippers were entirely of gold. When she appeared at the festival in this attire, they were all speechless with astonishment. The Prince danced only with her, and if any one else asked her to dance, he said, 'This is my partner.'

When night fell and she wanted to leave, the Prince was more desirous than ever to accompany her, but she darted away from him so quickly that he could not keep up with her. But the Prince had used a stratagem, and had caused the steps to be covered with cobbler's wax. The consequence was, that as the maiden sprang down them, her left slipper remained sticking there. The Prince took it up. It was small and dainty, and entirely made of gold.

The next morning he went with it to Ashenputtel's Father, and said to him, 'No other shall become my wife but she whose foot this golden slipper fits.'

The two sisters were delighted at that, for they both had beautiful feet. The eldest went into the room intending to try on the slipper, and her Mother stood beside her. But her great toe prevented her getting it on, her foot was too long.

Then her Mother handed her a knife, and said, 'Cut off

the toe ; when you are Queen you won't have to walk any more.'

The girl cut off her toe, forced her foot into the slipper, stifled her pain, and went out to the Prince. Then he took her up on his horse as his Bride, and rode away with her.

However, they had to pass the grave on the way, and there sat the two Doves on the hazel-tree, and cried :

'Prithee, look back, prithee, look back,
There's blood on the track,
The shoe is too small,
At home the true Bride is waiting thy call.'

Then he looked at her foot and saw how the blood was streaming from it. So he turned his horse round and carried the false Bride back to her home, and said that she was not the right one ; the second sister must try the shoe.

Then she went into the room, and succeeded in getting her toes into the shoe, but her heel was too big.

Then her Mother handed her a knife, and said, 'Cut a bit off your heel ; when you are Queen you won't have to walk any more.'

The maiden cut a bit off her heel, forced her foot into the shoe, stifled her pain, and went out to the Prince.

Then he took her up on his horse as his Bride, and rode off with her.

As they passed the grave, the two Doves were sitting on the hazel-tree, and crying :

'Prithee, look back, prithee, look back,
There's blood on the track,
The shoe is too small,
At home the true Bride is waiting thy call.'

He looked down at her foot and saw that it was streaming with blood, and there were deep red spots on her stockings. Then he turned his horse and brought the false Bride back to her home.

116

' This is not the right one either,' he said. ' Have you no other daughter ? '

' No,' said the man. ' There is only a daughter of my late wife's, a puny, stunted drudge, but she cannot possibly be the Bride.'

The Prince said that she must be sent for.

But the Mother answered, ' Oh no, she is much too dirty ; she mustn't be seen on any account.'

He was, however, absolutely determined to have his way, and they were obliged to summon Ashenputtel.

When she had washed her hands and face, she went up and curtsied to the Prince, who handed her the golden slipper.

Then she sat down on a bench, pulled off her wooden clog and put on the slipper, which fitted to a nicety.

And when she stood up and the Prince looked into her face, he recognised the beautiful maiden that he had danced with, and cried : ' This is the true Bride ! '

The Stepmother and the two sisters were dismayed and turned white with rage ; but he took Ashenputtel on his horse and rode off with her.

As they rode past the hazel-tree the two White Doves cried :

> ' Prithee, look back, prithee, look back,
>   No blood 's on the track,
>   The shoe 's *not* too small,
>   You carry the true Bride home to your hall.'

And when they had said this they both came flying down, and settled on Ashenputtel's shoulders, one on the right, and one on the left, and remained perched there.

When the wedding was going to take place, the two false sisters came and wanted to curry favour with her, and take part in her good fortune. As the bridal party was going to the church, the eldest was on the right side, the youngest on the left, and the Doves picked out one of the eyes of each of them.

117

Afterwards, when they were coming out of the church, the elder was on the left, the younger on the right, and the Doves picked out the other eye of each of them. And so for their wickedness and falseness they were punished with blindness for the rest of their days.

Tom Thumb

A POOR Peasant sat one evening by his hearth and poked the fire, while his Wife sat opposite spinning. He said : 'What a sad thing it is that we have no children ; our home is so quiet, while other folk's houses are noisy and cheerful.'

'Yes,' answered his Wife, and she sighed ; 'even if it were an only one, and if it were no bigger than my thumb, I should be quite content ; we would love it with all our hearts.'

Now, some time after this, she had a little boy who was strong and healthy, but was no bigger than a thumb. Then they said : 'Well, our wish is fulfilled, and, small as he is, we will love him dearly ' ; and because of his tiny stature they called him Tom Thumb. They let him want for nothing, yet still the child grew no bigger, but remained the same size as when he was born. Still, he looked out on the world with intelligent eyes, and soon showed himself a clever and agile creature, who was lucky in all he attempted.

One day, when the Peasant was preparing to go into the forest to cut wood, he said to himself : ' I wish I had some one to bring the cart after me.'

' O Father ! ' said Tom Thumb, ' I will soon bring it. You leave it to me ; it shall be there at the appointed time.'

Then the Peasant laughed, and said : ' How can that be ? You are much too small even to hold the reins.'

' That doesn't matter, if only Mother will harness the horse,' answered Tom. ' I will sit in his ear and tell him where to go.'

' Very well,' said the Father ; ' we will try it for once.'

When the time came, the Mother harnessed the horse, set Tom in his ear, and then the little creature called out ' Gee-up '

Tom Thumb.

and 'Whoa' in turn, and directed it where to go. It went quite well, just as though it were being driven by its master ; and they went the right way to the wood. Now it happened that while the cart was turning a corner, and Tom was calling to the horse, two strange men appeared on the scene.

'My goodness,' said one, 'what is this ? There goes a cart, and a driver is calling to the horse, but there is nothing to be seen.'

'There is something queer about this,' said the other ; 'we will follow the cart and see where it stops.'

The cart went on deep into the forest, and arrived quite safely at the place where the wood was cut.

When Tom spied his Father, he said : 'You see, Father, here I am with the cart ; now lift me down.' The Father held the horse with his left hand, and took his little son out of its ear with the right. Then Tom sat down quite happily on a straw.

When the two strangers noticed him, they did not know what to say for astonishment.

Then one drew the other aside, and said : 'Listen, that little creature might make our fortune if we were to show him in the town for money. We will buy him.'

So they went up to the Peasant, and said : 'Sell us the little man ; he shall be well looked after with us.'

'No,' said the Peasant ; 'he is the delight of my eyes, and I will not sell him for all the gold in the world.'

But Tom Thumb, when he heard the bargain, crept up by the folds of his Father's coat, placed himself on his shoulder, and whispered in his ear : 'Father, let me go ; I will soon come back again.'

Then his Father gave him to the two men for a fine piece of gold.

'Where will you sit ? ' they asked him.

'Oh, put me on the brim of your hat, then I can walk up and down and observe the neighbourhood without falling down.'

121

They did as he wished, and when Tom had said good-bye
to his Father, they went away with him.

They walked on till it was twilight, when the little man
said : ' You must lift me down.'

' Stay where you are,' answered the Man on whose head
he sat.

' No,' said Tom ; ' I will come down. Lift me down
immediately.'

The Man took off his hat and set the little creature in a
field by the wayside. He jumped and crept about for a time,
here and there among the sods, then slipped suddenly into a
mouse-hole which he had discovered.

' Good evening, gentlemen, just you go home without me,'
he called out to them in mockery.

They ran about and poked with sticks into the mouse-hole,
but all in vain. Tom crept further and further back, and,
as it soon got quite dark, they were forced to go home, full of
anger, and with empty purses.

When Tom noticed that they were gone, he crept out of
his underground hiding-place again. ' It is dangerous walking
in this field in the dark,' he said ; ' one might easily break
one's leg or one's neck.' Luckily, he came to an empty snail
shell. ' Thank goodness,' he said ; ' I can pass the night in
safety here,' and he sat down.

Not long after, just when he was about to go to sleep, he
heard two men pass by. One said : ' How shall we set about
stealing the rich parson's gold and silver ? '

' I can tell you,' interrupted Tom.

' What was that ? ' said one robber in a fright. ' I heard
some one speak.'

They remained standing and listened.

Then Tom spoke again : ' Take me with you and I will
help you.'

' Where are you ? ' they asked.

' Just look on the ground and see where the voice comes
from,' he answered.

When Tom had said good-bye to his Father they went away with him.

At last the thieves found him, and lifted him up. 'You little urchin, are *you* going to help us ?'

'Yes,' he said ; 'I will creep between the iron bars in the pastor's room, and will hand out to you what you want.'

'All right,' they said, 'we will see what you can do.'

When they came to the Parsonage, Tom crept into the room, but called out immediately with all his strength to the others : 'Do you want everything that is here ?'

The thieves were frightened, and said : 'Do speak softly, and don't wake any one.'

But Tom pretended not to understand, and called out again : 'What do you want ? Everything ?'

The Cook, who slept above, heard him and sat up in bed and listened. But the thieves were so frightened that they retreated a little way. At last they summoned up courage again, and thought to themselves, 'The little rogue wants to tease us.' So they came back and whispered to him : 'Now, do be serious, and hand us out something.'

Then Tom called out again, as loud as he could, 'I will give you everything if only you will hold out your hands.'

The Maid, who was listening intently, heard him quite distinctly, jumped out of bed, and stumbled to the door. The thieves turned and fled, running as though wild huntsmen were after them. But the Maid, seeing nothing, went to get a light. When she came back with it, Tom, without being seen, slipped out into the barn, and the Maid, after she had searched every corner and found nothing, went to bed again, thinking she had been dreaming with her eyes and ears open.

Tom Thumb climbed about in the hay, and found a splendid place to sleep. There he determined to rest till day came, and then to go home to his parents. But he had other experiences to go through first. This world is full of trouble and sorrow !

The Maid got up in the grey dawn to feed the cows. First she went into the barn, where she piled up an armful of hay, the very bundle in which poor Tom was asleep. But he slept so soundly that he knew nothing till he was almost in the mouth of the cow, who was eating him up with the hay.

' Heavens ! ' he said, ' however did I get into this mill ? ' but he soon saw where he was, and the great thing was to avoid being crushed between the cow's teeth. At last, whether he liked it or not, he had to go down the cow's throat.

' The windows have been forgotten in this house,' he said. ' The sun does not shine into it, and no light has been provided.'

Altogether he was very ill-pleased with his quarters, and, worst of all, more and more hay came in at the door, and the space grew narrower and narrower. At last he called out, in his fear, as loud as he could, ' Don't give me any more food. Don't give me any more food.'

The Maid was just milking the cow, and when she heard the same voice as in the night, without seeing any one, she was frightened, and slipped from her stool and spilt the milk. Then, in the greatest haste, she ran to her master, and said : ' Oh, your Reverence, the cow has spoken ! '

' You are mad,' he answered ; but he went into the stable himself to see what was happening.

Scarcely had he set foot in the cow-shed before Tom began again, ' Don't bring me any more food.'

Then the Pastor was terrified too, and thought that the cow must be bewitched ; so he ordered it to be killed. It was accordingly slaughtered, but the stomach, in which Tom was hidden, was thrown into the manure heap. Tom had the greatest trouble in working his way out. Just as he stuck out his head, a hungry Wolf ran by and snapped up the whole stomach with one bite. But still Tom did not lose courage. ' Perhaps the Wolf will listen to reason,' he said. So he called out, ' Dear Wolf, I know where you would find a magnificent meal.'

' Where is it to be had ? ' asked the Wolf.

' Why, in such and such a house,' answered Tom. ' You must squeeze through the grating of the store-room window,

125

and there you will find cakes, bacon, and sausages, as many as you can possibly eat'; and he went on to describe his father's house.

The Wolf did not wait to hear this twice, and at night forced himself in through the grating, and ate to his heart's content. When he **was** satisfied, he wanted to go away again ; but he had grown so fat that he could not get out the same way. Tom had reckoned on this, and began to make a great commotion inside the Wolf's body, struggling and screaming with all his might.

' Be quiet,' said the Wolf ; ' you will wake up the people of the house.'

' All very fine,' answered Tom. ' You have eaten your fill, and now I am going to make merry '; and he began to scream again with all his might.

At last his father and mother woke up, ran to the room, and looked through the crack of the door. When they saw a Wolf, they went away, and the husband fetched his axe, and the wife a scythe.

' You stay behind,' said the man, as they came into the room. ' If my blow does not kill him, you must attack him and rip up his body.'

When Tom Thumb heard his Father's voice, he called out : ' Dear Father, I am here, inside the Wolf's body.'

Full of joy, his Father cried, ' Heaven be praised ! our dear child is found again,' and he bade his wife throw aside the scythe that it might not injure Tom.

Then he gathered himself together, and struck the Wolf a blow on the head, so that it fell down lifeless. Then with knives and shears they ripped up the body, and took their little boy out.

' Ah,' said his Father, ' what trouble we have been in about you.'

' Yes, Father, I have travelled about the world, and I am thankful to breathe fresh air again.'

' Wherever have you been ? ' they asked.

'Down a mouse-hole, in a Cow's stomach, and in a Wolf's maw,' he answered ; ' and now I shall stay with you.'

' And we will never sell you again, for all the riches in the world,' they said, kissing and fondling their dear child.

Then they gave him food and drink, and had new clothes made for him, as his own had been spoilt in his travels.

Snowdrop

IT was the middle of winter, and the snowflakes were falling from the sky like feathers. Now, a Queen sat sewing at a window framed in black ebony, and as she sewed she looked out upon the snow. Suddenly she pricked her finger and three drops of blood fell on to the snow. And the red looked so lovely on the white that she thought to herself: ' If only I had a child as white as snow and as red as blood, and as black as the wood of the window frame ! ' Soon after, she had a daughter, whose hair was black as ebony, while her cheeks were red as blood, and her skin as white as snow ; so she was called Snowdrop. But when the child was born the Queen died. A year after the King took another wife. She was a handsome woman, but proud and overbearing, and could not endure that any one should surpass her in beauty. She had a magic looking-glass, and when she stood before it and looked at herself she used to say :

> ' Mirror, Mirror on the wall,
> Who is fairest of us all ? '

then the Glass answered,

> ' Queen, thou 'rt fairest of them all.'

Then she was content, for she knew that the Looking-glass spoke the truth.

But Snowdrop grew up and became more and more beautiful, so that when she was seven years old she was as beautiful as the day, and far surpassed the Queen. Once, when she asked her Glass,

128

SNOWDROP

'Mirror, Mirror on the wall,
Who is fairest of us all?'

it answered—

'Queen, thou art fairest here, I hold,
But Snowdrop is fairer a thousandfold.'

Then the Queen was horror-struck, and turned green and yellow with jealousy. From the hour that she saw Snowdrop her heart sank, and she hated the little girl.

The pride and envy of her heart grew like a weed, so that she had no rest day nor night. At last she called a Huntsman, and said: 'Take the child out into the wood; I will not set eyes on her again; you must kill her and bring me her lungs and liver as tokens.'

'Mirror, Mirror on the wall,
Who is fairest of us all?'

The Huntsman obeyed, and took Snowdrop out into the forest, but when he drew his hunting-knife and was preparing to plunge it into her innocent heart, she began to cry:

'Alas! dear Huntsman, spare my life, and I will run away into the wild forest and never come back again.'

And because of her beauty the Huntsman had pity on her and said, 'Well, run away, poor child.' Wild beasts will soon devour you, he thought, but still he felt as though a weight were lifted from his heart because he had

129

not been obliged to kill her. And as just at that moment a young fawn came leaping by, he pierced it and took the lungs and liver as tokens to the Queen. The Cook was ordered to serve them up in pickle, and the wicked Queen ate them thinking that they were Snowdrop's.

Now the poor child was alone in the great wood, with no living soul near, and she was so frightened that she knew not what to do. Then she began to run, and ran over the sharp stones and through the brambles, while the animals passed her by without harming her. She ran as far as her feet could carry her till it was nearly evening, when she saw a little house and went in to rest. Inside, everything was small, but as neat and clean as could be. A small table covered with a white cloth stood ready with seven small plates, and by every plate was a spoon, knife, fork, and cup. Seven little beds were ranged against the walls, covered with snow-white coverlets. As Snowdrop was very hungry and thirsty she ate a little bread and vegetable from each plate, and drank a little wine from each cup, for she did not want to eat up the whole of one portion. Then, being very tired, she lay down in one of the beds. She tried them all but none suited her; one was too short, another too long, all except the seventh, which was just right. She remained in it, said her prayers, and fell asleep.

When it was quite dark the masters of the house came in. They were seven Dwarfs, who used to dig in the mountains for ore. They kindled their lights, and as soon as they could see they noticed that some one had been there, for everything was not in the order in which they had left it.

The first said, ' Who has been sitting in my chair ? '
The second said, ' Who has been eating off my plate ? '
The third said, ' Who has been nibbling my bread ? '
The fourth said, ' Who has been eating my vegetables ? '
The fifth said, ' Who has been using my fork ? '
The sixth said, ' Who has been cutting with my knife ? '
The seventh said, ' Who has been drinking out of my cup ? '

130

Then the first looked and saw a slight impression on his bed, and said, 'Who has been treading on my bed?' The others came running up and said, 'And mine, and mine.'

In the evening the seven Dwarfs came back.

But the seventh, when he looked into his bed, saw Snowdrop, who lay there asleep. He called the others, who came up and cried out with astonishment, as they held their lights and

131

gazed at Snowdrop. 'Heavens! what a beautiful child,' they said, and they were so delighted that they did not wake her up but left her asleep in bed. And the seventh Dwarf slept with his comrades, an hour with each all through the night.

When morning came Snowdrop woke up, and when she saw the seven Dwarfs she was frightened.

But they were very kind and asked her name.

'I am called Snowdrop,' she answered.

'How did you get into our house?' they asked.

Then she told them how her stepmother had wished to get rid of her, how the Huntsman had spared her life, and how she had run all day till she had found the house.

Then the Dwarfs said, 'Will you look after our household, cook, make the beds, wash, sew and knit, and keep everything neat and clean? If so you shall stay with us and want for nothing.'

'Yes,' said Snowdrop, 'with all my heart'; and she stayed with them and kept the house in order.

In the morning they went to the mountain and searched for copper and gold, and in the evening they came back and then their meal had to be ready. All day the maiden was alone, and the good Dwarfs warned her and said, 'Beware of your stepmother, who will soon learn that you are here. Don't let any one in.'

But the Queen, having, as she imagined, eaten Snowdrop's liver and lungs, and feeling certain that she was the fairest of all, stepped in front of her Glass, and asked—

> 'Mirror, Mirror on the wall,
> Who is fairest of us all?'

the Glass answered as usual—

> 'Queen, thou art fairest here, I hold,
> But Snowdrop over the fells,
> Who with the seven Dwarfs dwells,
> Is fairer still a thousandfold.'

132

She was dismayed, for she knew that the Glass told no lies, and she saw that the Hunter had deceived her and that Snowdrop still lived. Accordingly she began to wonder afresh how she might compass her death; for as long as she was not the fairest in the land her jealous heart left her no rest. At last she thought of a plan. She dyed her face and dressed up like an old Pedlar, so that she was quite unrecognisable. In this guise she crossed over the seven mountains to the home of the seven Dwarfs and called out, ' Wares for sale.'

Snowdrop peeped out of the window and said, ' Good-day, mother, what have you got to sell ? '

' Good wares, fine wares,' she answered, ' laces of every colour '; and she held out one which was made of gay plaited silk.

' I may let the honest woman in,' thought Snowdrop, and she unbolted the door and bought the pretty lace.

' Child,' said the Old Woman, ' what a sight you are, I will lace you properly for once.'

Snowdrop made no objection, and placed herself before the Old Woman to let her lace her with the new lace. But the Old Woman laced so quickly and tightly that she took away Snow-drop's breath and she fell down as though dead.

' Now I am the fairest,' she said to herself, and hurried away.

Not long after the seven Dwarfs came home, and were horror-struck when they saw their dear little Snowdrop lying on the floor without stirring, like one dead. When they saw she was laced too tight they cut the lace, whereupon she began to breathe and soon came back to life again. When the Dwarfs heard what had happened, they said that the old Pedlar was no other than the wicked Queen. ' Take care not to let any one in when we are not here,' they said.

Now the wicked Queen, as soon as she got home, went to the Glass and asked—

' Mirror, Mirror on the wall,
Who is fairest of us all ? '

and it answered as usual—

> 'Queen, thou art fairest here, I hold,
> But Snowdrop over the fells,
> Who with the seven Dwarfs dwells,
> Is fairer still a thousandfold.'

When she heard it all her blood flew to her heart, so enraged was she, for she knew that Snowdrop had come back to life again. Then she thought to herself, ' I must plan something which will put an end to her.' By means of witchcraft, in which she was skilled, she made a poisoned comb. Next she disguised herself and took the form of a different Old Woman. She crossed the mountains and came to the home of the seven Dwarfs, and knocked at the door calling out, ' Good wares to sell.'

Snowdrop looked out of the window and said, ' Go away, I must not let any one in.'

' At least you may look,' answered the Old Woman, and she took the poisoned comb and held it up.

The child was so pleased with it that she let herself be beguiled, and opened the door.

When she had made a bargain the Old Woman said, ' Now I will comb your hair properly for once.'

Poor Snowdrop, suspecting no evil, let the Old Woman have her way, but scarcely was the poisoned comb fixed in her hair than the poison took effect, and the maiden fell down unconscious.

' You paragon of beauty,' said the wicked woman, ' now it is all over with you,' and she went away.

Happily it was near the time when the seven Dwarfs came home. When they saw Snowdrop lying on the ground as though dead, they immediately suspected her stepmother, and searched till they found the poisoned comb. No sooner had they removed it than Snowdrop came to herself again and related what had happened. They warned her again to be on her guard, and to open the door to no one.

134

SNOWDROP

When she got home the Queen stood before her Glass and said—

> 'Mirror, Mirror on the wall,
> Who is fairest of us all?'

and it answered as usual—

> 'Queen, thou art fairest here, I hold,
> But Snowdrop over the fells,
> Who with the seven Dwarfs dwells,
> Is fairer still a thousandfold.'

When she heard the Glass speak these words she trembled and quivered with rage, 'Snowdrop shall die,' she said, 'even if it cost me my own life.' Thereupon she went into a secret room, which no one ever entered but herself, and made a poisonous apple. Outwardly it was beautiful to look upon, with rosy cheeks, and every one who saw it longed for it, but whoever ate of it was certain to die. When the apple was ready she dyed her face and dressed herself like an old Peasant Woman and so crossed the seven hills to the Dwarfs' home. There she knocked.

Snowdrop put her head out of the window and said, 'I must not let any one in, the seven Dwarfs have forbidden me.'

'It is all the same to me,' said the Peasant Woman. 'I shall soon get rid of my apples. There, I will give you one.'

'No; I must not take anything.'

'Are you afraid of poison?' said the woman. 'See, I will cut the apple in half : you eat the red side and I will keep the other.'

Now the apple was so cunningly painted that the red half alone was poisoned. Snowdrop longed for the apple, and when she saw the Peasant Woman eating she could hold out no longer, stretched out her hand and took the poisoned half. Scarcely had she put a bit into her mouth than she fell dead to the ground.

The Queen looked with a fiendish glance, and laughed aloud and said, 'White as snow, red as blood, and black as ebony,

135

this time the Dwarfs cannot wake you up again.' And when she got home and asked the Looking-glass—

> 'Mirror, Mirror on the wall,
> Who is fairest of us all?'

it answered at last—

> 'Queen, thou 'rt fairest of them all.'

Then her jealous heart was at rest, as much at rest as a jealous heart can be. The Dwarfs, when they came at evening, found Snowdrop lying on the ground and not a breath escaped her lips, and she was quite dead. They lifted her up and looked to see whether any poison was to be found, unlaced her dress, combed her hair, washed her with wine and water, but it was no use; their dear child was dead. They laid her on a bier, and all seven sat down and bewailed her and lamented over her for three whole days. Then they prepared to bury her, but she looked so fresh and living, and still had such beautiful rosy cheeks, that they said, 'We cannot bury her in the dark earth.' And so they had a transparent glass coffin made, so that she could be seen from every side, laid her inside and wrote on it in letters of gold her name and how she was a King's daughter. Then they set the coffin out on the mountain, and one of them always stayed by and watched it. And the birds came too and mourned for Snowdrop, first an owl, then a raven, and lastly a dove.

Now Snowdrop lay a long, long time in her coffin, looking as though she were asleep. It happened that a Prince was wandering in the wood, and came to the home of the seven Dwarfs to pass the night. He saw the coffin on the mountain and lovely Snowdrop inside, and read what was written in golden letters. Then he said to the Dwarfs, 'Let me have the coffin; I will give you whatever you like for it.'

But they said, 'We will not give it up for all the gold of the world.'

Then he said, 'Then give it to me as a gift, for I cannot

136

The Dwarfs, when they came in the evening, found Snowdrop lying on the ground.

live without Snowdrop to gaze upon ; and I will honour and reverence it as my dearest treasure.'

When he had said these words the good Dwarfs pitied him and gave him the coffin.

The Prince bade his servants carry it on their shoulders. Now it happened that they stumbled over some brushwood, and the shock dislodged the piece of apple from Snowdrop's throat. In a short time she opened her eyes, lifted the lid of the coffin, sat up and came back to life again completely.

' O Heaven ! where am I ? ' she asked.

The Prince, full of joy, said, ' You are with me,' and he related what had happened, and then said, ' I love you better than all the world ; come with me to my father's castle and be my wife.'

Snowdrop agreed and went with him, and their wedding was celebrated with great magnificence. Snowdrop's wicked stepmother was invited to the feast; and when she had put on her fine clothes she stepped to her Glass and asked—

'Mirror, Mirror on the wall,
Who is fairest of us all ?'

The Glass answered—

'Queen, thou art fairest here, I hold,
The young Queen fairer a thousandfold.'

Then the wicked woman uttered a curse, and was so terribly frightened that she didn't know what to do. Yet she had no rest : she felt obliged to go and see the young Queen. And when she came in she recognised Snowdrop, and stood stock still with fear and terror. But iron slippers were heated over the fire, and were soon brought in with tongs and put before her. And she had to step into the red-hot shoes and dance till she fell down dead.

Jealousy over comes her.

138

King Thrushbeard

THERE was once a King who had a Daughter. She was more beautiful than words can tell, but at the same time so proud and haughty that no man who came to woo her was good enough for her. She turned away one after another, and even mocked them.

One day her father ordered a great feast to be given, and invited to it all the marriageable young men from far and near.

They were all placed in a row, according to their rank and position. First came Kings, then Princes, then Dukes, Earls, and Barons.

The Princess was led through the ranks, but she had some fault to find with all of them.

One was too stout. ' That barrel ! ' she said. The next was too tall. ' Long and lean is no good ! ' The third was too short. ' Short and stout, can't turn about ! ' The fourth was too white. ' Pale as death ! ' The fifth was too red. ' Turkey-cock ! ' The sixth was not straight. ' Oven-dried ! '

So there was something against each of them. But she made specially merry over one good King, who stood quite at the head of the row, and whose chin was a little hooked.

' Why ! ' she cried, ' he has a chin like the beak of a thrush.'

After that, he was always called ' King Thrushbeard.'

When the old King saw that his Daughter only made fun of them, and despised all the suitors who were assembled, he was very angry, and swore that the first beggar who came to the door should be her husband.

A few days after, a wandering Musician began to sing at the window, hoping to receive charity.

When the King heard him, he said : ' Let him be brought in.'

The Musician came in, dressed in dirty rags, and sang to the King and his Daughter, and when he had finished, he begged alms of them.

The King said : ' Your song has pleased me so much, that I will give you my Daughter to be your wife.'

The Princess was horror-stricken. But the King said : ' I have sworn an oath to give you to the first beggar who came ; and I will keep my word.'

No entreaties were of any avail. A Parson was brought, and she had to marry the Musician there and then.

When the marriage was completed, the King said : ' Now you are a beggar-woman, you can't stay in my castle any longer. You must go away with your Husband.'

The Beggar took her by the hand and led her away, and she was obliged to go with him on foot.

When they came to a big wood, she asked :

'Ah! who is the Lord of this forest so fine?'
'It belongs to King Thrushbeard. It might have been thine,
If his Queen you had been.'
'Ah! sad must I sing!
I would I'd accepted the hand of the King.'

After that they reached a great meadow, and she asked again :

'Ah! who is the Lord of these meadows so fine?'
'They belong to King Thrushbeard, and would have been thine,
If his Queen you had been.'
'Ah! sad must I sing!
I would I'd accepted the love of the King.'

Then they passed through a large town, and again she asked :

'Ah! who is the Lord of this city so fine?'
'It belongs to King Thrushbeard, and it might have been thine,
If his Queen you had been.'
'Ah! sad must I sing!
I would I'd accepted the heart of the King.

The Beggar took her by the hand and led her away.

'It doesn't please me at all,' said the Musician, 'that you are always wishing for another husband. Am I not good enough for you?'

At last they came to a miserable little hovel, and she said:

'Ah, heavens! what's this house, so mean and small?
This wretched little hut's no house at all.'

The Musician answered: 'This is my house, and yours; where we are to live together.'

The door was so low that she had to stoop to get in.

'Where are the servants?' asked the Princess.

'Servants indeed!' answered the Beggar. 'Whatever you want done, you must do for yourself. Light the fire, and put the kettle on to make my supper. I am very tired.'

But the Princess knew nothing about lighting fires or cooking, and to get it done at all, the Beggar had to do it himself.

When they had finished their humble fare, they went to bed. But in the morning the Man made her get up very early to do the housework.

They lived like this for a few days, till they had eaten up all their store of food.

Then the Man said: 'Wife, this won't do any longer; we can't live here without working. You shall make baskets.'

So he went out and cut some osiers, and brought them home. She began to weave them, but the hard osiers bruised her tender hands.

'I see that won't do,' said the Beggar. 'You had better spin; perhaps you can manage that.'

So she sat down and tried to spin, but the harsh yarn soon cut her delicate fingers and made them bleed.

'Now you see,' said the Man, 'what a good-for-nothing you are. I have made a bad bargain in you. But I will try to start a trade in earthenware. You must sit in the market and offer your goods for sale.'

'Alas!' she thought, 'if any of the people from my father's kingdom come and see me sitting in the market-place, offering

142

goods for sale, they will scoff at me. But it was no good. She had to obey, unless she meant to die of hunger.

All went well the first time. The people willingly bought her wares because she was so handsome, and they paid what she asked them—nay, some even gave her the money and left her the pots as well.

They lived on the gains as long as they lasted, and then the Man laid in a new stock of wares.

She took her seat in a corner of the market, set out her crockery about her, and began to cry her wares.

Suddenly, a drunken Hussar came galloping up, and rode right in among the pots, breaking them into thousands of bits.

She began to cry, and was so frightened that she did not know what to do. 'Oh! what will become of me?' she cried. 'What will my Husband say to me?' She ran home, and told him her misfortune.

'Who would ever think of sitting at the corner of the market with crockery?' he said. 'Stop that crying. I see you are no manner of use for any decent kind of work. I have been to our King's palace, and asked if they do not want a kitchen wench, and they have promised to try you. You will get your victuals free, at any rate.'

So the Princess became a kitchen wench, and had to wait upon the Cook and do all the dirty work. She fixed a pot into each of her pockets, and in them took home her share of the scraps and leavings, and upon these they lived.

It so happened that the marriage of the eldest Princess just then took place, and the poor Woman went upstairs and stood behind the door to peep at all the splendour.

When the rooms were lighted up, and she saw the guests streaming in, one more beautiful than the other, and the scene grew more and more brilliant, she thought, with a heavy heart, of her sad fate. She cursed the pride and haughtiness which had been the cause of her humiliation, and of her being brought to such depths.

Every now and then the Servants would throw her bits from

the savoury dishes they were carrying away from the feast, and these she put into her pots to take home with her.

All at once the King's son came in. He was dressed in silk and velvet, and he had a golden chain round his neck.

When he saw the beautiful Woman standing at the door, he seized her by the hand, and wanted to dance with her.

But she shrank and refused, because she saw that it was King Thrushbeard, who had been one of the suitors for her hand, and whom she had most scornfully driven away.

Her resistance was no use, and he dragged her into the hall. The string by which her pockets were suspended broke. Down fell the pots, and the soup and savoury morsels were spilt all over the floor.

When the guests saw it, they burst into shouts of mocking laughter.

She was so ashamed, that she would gladly have sunk into the earth. She rushed to the door, and tried to escape, but on the stairs a Man stopped her and brought her back.

When she looked at him, it was no other than King Thrushbeard again.

He spoke kindly to her, and said : 'Do not be afraid. I and the Beggar-Man, who lived in the poor little hovel with you, are one and the same. For love of you I disguised myself ; and I was also the Hussar who rode among your pots. All this I did to bend your proud spirit, and to punish you for the haughtiness with which you mocked me.'

She wept bitterly, and said : 'I was very wicked, and I am not worthy to be your wife.'

But he said : 'Be happy! Those evil days are over. Now we will celebrate our true wedding.'

The waiting-women came and put rich clothing upon her, and her Father, with all his Court, came and wished her joy on her marriage with King Thrushbeard.

Then, in truth, her happiness began. I wish we had been there to see it, you and I.

The Elves and the Shoemaker

THERE was once a Shoemaker who, through no fault of his own, had become so poor that at last he had only leather enough left for one pair of shoes. At evening he cut out the shoes which he intended to begin upon the next morning, and since he had a good conscience, he lay down quietly, said his prayers, and fell asleep.

In the morning when he had said his prayers, and was preparing to sit down to work, he found the pair of shoes standing finished on his table. He was amazed, and could not understand it in the least.

He took the shoes in his hand to examine them more closely. They were so neatly sewn that not a stitch was out of place, and were as good as the work of a master-hand.

Soon after a purchaser came in, and as he was much pleased with the shoes, he paid more than the ordinary price for them, so that the Shoemaker was able to buy leather for two pairs of shoes with the money.

He cut them out in the evening, and next day, with fresh courage, was about to go to work ; but he had no need to, for when he got up, the shoes were finished, and buyers were not lacking. These gave him so much money that he was able to buy leather for four pairs of shoes.

Early next morning he found the four pairs finished, and so it went on ; what he cut out at evening was finished in the morning, so that he was soon again in comfortable circumstances, and became a well-to-do man.

Now it happened one evening, not long before Christmas, when he had cut out some shoes as usual, that he said to his

Wife : ' How would it be if we were to sit up to-night to see who it is that lends us such a helping hand ? '

The Wife agreed, lighted a candle, and they hid themselves in the corner of the room behind the clothes which were hanging there.

At midnight came two little naked men who sat down at the Shoemaker's table, took up the cut-out work, and began with their tiny fingers to stitch, sew, and hammer so neatly and quickly, that the Shoemaker could not believe his eyes. They did not stop till everything was quite finished, and stood complete on the table ; then they ran swiftly away.

The next day the Wife said : ' The little men have made us rich, and we ought to show our gratitude. They were running about with nothing on, and must freeze with cold. Now I will make them little shirts, coats, waistcoats, and hose, and will even knit them a pair of stockings, and you shall make them each a pair of shoes.'

The Husband agreed, and at evening, when they had everything ready, they laid out the presents on the table, and hid themselves to see how the little men would behave.

At midnight they came skipping in, and were about to set to work ; but, instead of the leather ready cut out, they found the charming little clothes.

At first they were surprised, then excessively delighted. With the greatest speed they put on and smoothed down the pretty clothes, singing :

> ' Now we 're boys so fine and neat,
>   Why cobble more for other's feet ? '

Then they hopped and danced about, and leapt over chairs and tables and out at the door. Henceforward, they came back no more, but the Shoemaker fared well as long as he lived, and had good luck in all his undertakings.

146

The Twelve
Dancing Princesses

THERE was once a King who had twelve daughters, each more beautiful than the other. They slept together in a hall where their beds stood close to one another; and at night, when they had gone to bed, the King locked the door and bolted it. But when he unlocked it in the morning, he noticed that their shoes had been danced to pieces, and nobody could explain how it happened. So the King sent out a proclamation saying that any one who could discover where the Princesses did their night's dancing should choose one of them to be his wife and should reign after his death; but whoever presented himself, and failed to make the discovery after three days and nights, was to forfeit his life.

A Prince soon presented himself and offered to take the risk. He was well received, and at night was taken into a room adjoining the hall where the Princesses slept. His bed was made up there, and he was to watch and see where they went to dance; so that they could not do anything, or go anywhere else, the door of his room was left open too. But the eyes of the King's son grew heavy, and he fell asleep. When he woke up in the morning all the twelve had been dancing, for the soles of their shoes were full of holes. The second and third evenings passed with the same results, and then the Prince found no mercy, and his head was cut off.

147

Many others came after him and offered to take the risk, but they all had to lose their lives.

Now it happened that a poor Soldier, who had been wounded and could no longer serve, found himself on the road to the town where the King lived. There he fell in with an old woman who asked him where he intended to go.

'I really don't know, myself,' he said ; and added, in fun, 'I should like to discover where the King's daughters dance their shoes into holes, and after that to become King.'

'That is not so difficult,' said the old woman. 'You must not drink the wine which will be brought to you in the evening, but must pretend to be fast asleep.' Whereupon she gave him a short cloak, saying : 'When you wear this you will be invisible, and then you can slip out after the Twelve Princesses.'

As soon as the Soldier heard this good advice he took it up seriously, plucked up courage, appeared before the King, and offered himself as suitor. He was as well received as the others, and was dressed in royal garments.

In the evening, when bed-time came, he was conducted to the ante-room. As he was about to go to bed the eldest Princess appeared, bringing him a cup of wine ; but he had fastened a sponge under his chin and let the wine run down into it, so that he did not drink one drop. Then he lay down, and when he had been quiet a little while he began to snore as though in the deepest sleep.

The Twelve Princesses heard him, and laughed. The eldest said : 'He, too, must forfeit his life.'

Then they got up, opened cupboards, chests, and cases, and brought out their beautiful dresses. They decked themselves before the glass, skipping about and revelling in the prospect of the dance. Only the youngest sister said : 'I don't know what it is. You may rejoice, but I feel so strange ; a misfortune is certainly hanging over us.'

'You are a little goose,' answered the eldest ; 'you are always frightened. Have you forgotten how many Princes

148

have come here in vain ? Why, I need not have given the Soldier a sleeping draught at all ; the blockhead would never have awakened.'

When they were all ready they looked at the Soldier ; but his eyes were shut and he did not stir. So they thought they would soon be quite safe. Then the eldest went up to one of the beds and knocked on it ; it sank into the earth, and they descended through the opening, one after another, the eldest first.

The Soldier, who had noticed everything, did not hesitate long, but threw on his cloak and went down behind the youngest. Half-way down he trod on her dress. She was frightened, and said : ' What was that ? who is holding on to my dress ? '

' Don't be so foolish. You must have caught on a nail,' said the eldest. Then they went right down, and when they got quite underground, they stood in a marvellously beautiful avenue of trees ; all the leaves were silver, and glittered and shone.

The Soldier thought, ' I must take away some token with me.' And as he broke off a twig, a sharp crack came from the tree.

The youngest cried out, ' All is not well ; did you hear that sound ? '

' Those are triumphal salutes, because we shall soon have released our Princes,' said the eldest.

Next they came to an avenue where all the leaves were of gold, and, at last, into a third, where they were of shining diamonds. From both these he broke off a twig, and there was a crack each time which made the youngest Princess start with terror ; but the eldest maintained that the sounds were only triumphal salutes. They went on faster, and came to a great lake. Close to the bank lay twelve little boats, and in every boat sat a handsome Prince. They had expected the Twelve Princesses, and each took one with him ; but the Soldier seated himself by the youngest.

Then said the Prince, 'I don't know why, but the boat is much heavier to-day, and I am obliged to row with all my strength to get it along.'

'I wonder why it is,' said the youngest, 'unless, perhaps, it is the hot weather; it is strangely hot.'

On the opposite side of the lake stood a splendid brightly-lighted castle, from which came the sound of the joyous music of trumpets and drums. They rowed across, and every Prince danced with his love; and the Soldier danced too, unseen. If one of the Princesses held a cup of wine he drank out of it, so that it was empty when she lifted it to her lips. This frightened the youngest one, but the eldest always silenced her. They danced till three next morning, when their shoes were danced into holes, and they were obliged to stop. The Princes took them back across the lake, and this time the Soldier took his seat beside the eldest. On the bank they said farewell to their Princes, and promised to come again the next night. When they got to the steps, the Soldier ran on ahead, lay down in bed, and when the twelve came lagging by, slowly and wearily, he began to snore again, very loud, so that they said, 'We are quite safe as far as he is concerned.' Then they took off their beautiful dresses, put them away, placed the worn-out shoes under their beds, and lay down.

The next morning the Soldier determined to say nothing, but to see the wonderful doings again. So he went with them the second and third nights. Everything was just the same as the first time, and they danced each time till their shoes were in holes; but the third time the Soldier took away a wine-cup as a token.

When the appointed hour came for his answer, he took the three twigs and the cup with him and went before the King. The Twelve Princesses stood behind the door listening to hear what he would say. When the King put the question, 'Where did my daughters dance their shoes to pieces in the night?' he answered: 'With twelve Princes in an underground castle.' Then he produced the tokens.

On the opposite side of the lake stood a splendid brightly-lighted Castle.

The King sent for his daughters and asked them whether the Soldier had spoken the truth. As they saw that they were betrayed, and would gain nothing by lies, they were obliged to admit all. Thereupon the King asked the Soldier which one he would choose as his wife. He answered : 'I am no longer young, give me the eldest.'

So the wedding was celebrated that very day, and the kingdom was promised to him on the King's death. But for every night which the Princes had spent in dancing with the Princesses a day was added to their time of enchantment.

The Seven Ravens

THERE was once a Man who had seven sons, but never a daughter, however much he wished for one.

At last, however, he had a daughter.

His joy was great, but the child was small and delicate, and, on account of its weakness, it was to be christened at home.

The Father sent one of his sons in haste to the spring to fetch some water; the other six ran with him, and because each of them wanted to be the first to draw the water, between them the pitcher fell into the brook.

There they stood and didn't know what to do, and not one of them ventured to go home.

As they did not come back, their Father became impatient, and said : ' Perhaps the young rascals are playing about, and have forgotten it altogether.'

He became anxious lest his little girl should die unbaptized, and in hot vexation, he cried : ' I wish the youngsters would all turn into Ravens ! '

Scarcely were the words uttered, when he heard a whirring in the air above his head, and, looking upwards, he saw seven coal-black Ravens flying away.

The parents could not undo the spell, and were very sad about the loss of their seven sons, but they consoled themselves in some measure with their dear little daughter, who soon became strong, and every day more beautiful.

For a long time she was unaware that she had had any brothers, for her parents took care not to mention it.

However, one day by chance she heard some people saying about her : ' Oh yes, the girl 's pretty enough ; but you know she is really to blame for the misfortune to her seven brothers.'

Then she became very sad, and went to her father and mother and asked if she had ever had any brothers, and what had become of them.

The parents could no longer conceal the secret. They said, however, that what had happened was by the decree of heaven, and that her birth was merely the innocent occasion.

But the little girl could not get the matter off her conscience for a single day, and thought that she was bound to release her brothers again. She had no peace or quiet until she had secretly set out, and gone forth into the wide world to trace her brothers, wherever they might be, and to free them, let it cost what it might.

She took nothing with her but a little ring as a remembrance of her parents, a loaf of bread against hunger, a pitcher of water against thirst, and a little chair in case of fatigue. She kept ever going on and on until she came to the end of the world.

Then she came to the Sun, but it was hot and terrible, it devoured little children. She ran hastily away to the Moon, but it was too cold, and, moreover, dismal and dreary. And when the child was looking at it, it said : ' I smell, I smell man's flesh ! '

Then she quickly made off, and came to the Stars, and they were kind and good, and every one sat on his own special seat.

But the Morning Star stood up, and gave her a little bone, and said : ' Unless you have this bone, you cannot open the glass mountain, and in the glass mountain are your brothers.'

The girl took the bone, and wrapped it up carefully in a little kerchief, and went on again until she came to the glass mountain.

The gate was closed, and she meant to get out the little bone. But when she undid the kerchief it was empty, and she had lost the good Star's present.

How, now, was she to set to work ? She was determined to rescue her brothers, but had no key to open the glass mountain.

154

The good little Sister cut off her own tiny finger, fitted it into
the lock, and succeeded in opening it.

The good little sister took a knife and cut off her own tiny finger, fitted it into the keyhole, and succeeded in opening the lock.

When she had entered. she met a Dwarf. who said : ' My child, what are you looking for ? '

' I am looking for my brothers, the Seven Ravens,' she answered.

The Dwarf said : ' My masters, the Ravens, are not at home ; but if you like to wait until they come, please to walk in.'

Thereupon the Dwarf brought in the Ravens' supper, on seven little plates, and in seven little cups, and the little sister ate a crumb or two from each of the little plates, and took a sip from each of the little cups, but she let the ring she had brought with her fall into the last little cup.

All at once a whirring and crying were heard in the air ; then the Dwarf said : ' Now my masters the Ravens are coming home.'

Then they came in, and wanted to eat and drink, and began to look about for their little plates and cups.

But they said one after another : ' Halloa ! who has been eating off my plate ? Who has been drinking out of my cup ? There has been some human mouth here.'

When she entered she met a Dwarf.

And when the seventh drank to the bottom of his cup, the ring rolled up against his lips.

He looked at it, and recognised it as a ring belonging to his father and mother, and said : ' God grant that our sister may be here, and that we may be delivered.'

156

THE SEVEN RAVENS

As the maiden was standing behind the door listening, she heard the wish and came forward, and then all the Ravens got back their human form again.

And they embraced and kissed one another, and went joyfully home.

The Ravens coming home.

AFTERWORD

Folk and fairy tales are as old as humankind—and no collection is as enduring and beloved as the stories collected by the Brothers Grimm. So well-known are these tales that it is a rare child who cannot tell you the names of the girl in a red cape on her way to visit her grandmother, or the brother and sister who discover a witch's house, or the young princess who is befriended by a band of dwarfs. Though many editions of these fairy tales have been published in the nearly two centuries since they first appeared, there have been few illustrators who have captured the magic, drama, and humor of these stories as well as the celebrated English artist Arthur Rackham.

Jacob and Wilhelm Grimm were born in 1785 and 1786, respectively, in a small town near Frankfurt, Germany. Unusually close throughout their lives, they shared rooms as children and then again as law students at Marburg University; in their later years they lived in the same house and shared adjacent studies. But what brought them to world prominence was their shared passion for collecting German folktales. Though the brothers originally began collecting these stories with the hopes of eventually writing a history of German literature, their friend Achim von Arnim, who in 1805 had published a collection of German folk-songs, persuaded them to publish as a separate book the fairy tales they had gathered. As a result, the first volume of the *Kinder- und Hausmärchen (Nursery and Household Tales)* was issued in 1812 and the second volume followed shortly after, in 1814.

The *Kinder- und Hausmärchen* soon brought Jacob and Wilhelm fame in both Germany and abroad. The stories, mostly gathered from oral sources, revealed a previously unrecorded wealth of fairy tales and folk stories that were both educational and entertaining. And yet the

158

brothers did not at first look upon their collection as amusement, and certainly not as a book for children. The first edition of the *Kinder- und Hausmärchen* had no illustrations and included the long introduction and numerous notes one would expect in a scholarly work.

However, when the first English translation was published in 1823, it featured illustrations by the prominent British artist George Cruikshank and was clearly marketed as a collection for children. Apparently the brothers then recognized the potential in presenting their stories to young people and soon issued an inexpensive children's illustrated edition in Germany featuring fifty of their best stories. By the end of the nineteenth century the fairy tales of the Brothers Grimm had become a must for every child's library.

One of the first illustrated editions of the twentieth century was by an up-and-coming British illustrator named Arthur Rackham. Born in 1867 in south London and one of twelve children, he described his own boyhood as being "spent in a noisy, merry, busy little community of work and play." Showing an early talent for caricatures and fantasy drawings, young Arthur's interest in art was carefully encouraged in school. However, he left school at the age of sixteen due to frail health, and took a six-month voyage to Australia. While his health improved, he sketched continuously, and made the decision to become a professional artist.

Returning to London, Rackham enrolled in the Lambeth School of Art, taking classes at night and working as a clerk in an insurance office during the day for the next seven years. His pictures began to appear in various journals and books, and then the children's magazine *Little Folks*. Fearing that photography would replace illustrations in journals, he focused on illustrating fanciful tales where his vivid imagination could run free. In the late 1890s he began to focus on creating beautiful editions of such classics as *The Ingoldsby Legends* (1898), *Tales from Shakespeare* (1899), *Gulliver's Travels* (1900), and *Fairy Tales of the Brothers Grimm* (1900), for which he created one hundred black-and-white drawings. Though all these books contained his highly acclaimed pen-and-ink drawings, none contained the color plates for which he would soon become world famous.

Then, with the introduction of the four-color printing process, Rackham was offered the opportunity to do a truly lavish illustrated edition of a classic. When his *Rip Van Winkle* was issued in 1905 with fifty-one color plates, it was universally hailed as a masterpiece.

AFTERWORD

And with the publication of *Peter Pan in Kensington Gardens* (1906) and *Alice's Adventures in Wonderland* (1907), Rackham firmly established his reputation as one of the world's leading book illustrators.

Rackham continued to be fascinated by the fairy tales of the Brothers Grimm, however. Throughout this period he worked on his drawings for the tales—redrawing some in color, adding new ones in color and black-and-white, and in general revising the whole suite of illustrations. If you look through the illustrations in this book, you will notice that while many of the drawings are dated 1900, the color plates are dated anywhere from 1902 through 1909—and some are even dated twice. Finally, in 1909, a new Rackham edition of Grimm was issued. Far grander than the 1900 edition, it was simply titled *Grimm's Fairy Tales* and featured forty color plates and fifty-five line drawings.

Though a critical success, this deluxe edition proved physically unwieldy—not to mention expensive. In fact, today the 1909 edition is quite rare since most fell apart due to the book's excessive weight. This is why in 1920 the collection was reissued in two volumes titled *Hansel & Gretel & Other Tales* and *Snowdrop & Other Tales*. Each volume contained twenty color plates and twenty-eight line drawings. The trouble with this arrangement was that the most popular stories were divided between volumes, and so in order to have all of those beloved tales, one had to buy both. In creating this new edition, we selected twenty-two of the best-known Grimm stories and combined them with twenty-one of Arthur Rackham's fantastic color plates and twenty-eight of his marvelous pen-and-ink drawings. The result is the best of both Rackham and Grimm in one glorious volume.

It is only fitting that as we enter the twenty-first century, we preserve and enjoy for ourselves, our children, and future generations this remarkable pairing of great talents that have inspired so many generations that came before.

—Peter Glassman